Advance P
Frogs for W

'An enthralling novel, and a remarkable imaginative feat – the narrative voice is wholly convincing, and utterly compelling. Seán Farrell is a magical writer, and his name is one to conjure with.'

JOHN BANVILLE,
Booker Prize-winning author of *The Sea*

'*Frogs for Watchdogs* is a profound and moving novel that brings into light, with astonishing precision, the bewildering intensity of being young. This is a unique and remarkable work. So strange and utterly convincing.

ADRIAN DUNCAN,
author of *The Geometer Lobachevsky*

'This is a very special novel. It is rare to read such a convincing child's voice, and rarer still to see the world through his eyes in such an intense, visceral way. His anxiety and his desire to protect his mother are heart-rending, his belief in the power of his imagination terrifying. Each character is fully realised, from the kooky mother to Mrs Lynch with her sneaky Majors. As for Jerry Drain . . . his patience and dignity slayed me.'

LOUISE KENNEDY,
author of *Trespasses*

'This book felled me. Captures the burden the young carry; their vigilance in a time of lost fathers, lost footing and lost language. I loved every character: displaced, marginalised and broken – they save one another. This is a beautiful novel. I couldn't put it down.'

UNA MANNION,
author of *A Crooked Tree*

'A bewitching portrayal of the sweet, complicated consciousness of a young boy who lives in a kingdom of his own imagining and of his own endearing but perplexing paranoia. Wise and precise, nuanced and frank, Seán Farrell's fiction works on several levels at once, creating pleasure, intrigue and unease.'

BELINDA McKEON,
author of *Tender*

'*Frogs for Watchdogs* is a beautiful novel. The first three quarters are laden with tension and dread but this dense foreboding lightens and lifts towards the closing sections as we stand back from the story and witness, with growing joy, a wonderful, ineluctable slide towards love. I love the unforced narrative voice and its gorgeous contortions and confections; his innocent yet curiously ancient-feeling observations on the land around him and the people in it. A stunning novel that will live long in my imagination.'

DONAL RYAN,
author of *The Queen of Dirt Island*

FROGS FOR WATCHDOGS

Seán Farrell

NEW ISLAND

FROGS FOR WATCHDOGS
First published in 2025 by
New Island Books
Glenshesk House
10 Richview Office Park
Clonskeagh
Dublin D14 V8C4
Republic of Ireland
newisland.ie

Print ISBN: 978-1-84840-935-4
eBook ISBN: 978-1-84840-936-1

British Library Cataloguing in Publication Data. A CIP catalogue record for this book is available from the British Library.

Set in 11.75 on 17pt in Adobe Caslon Pro

Typeset by JVR Creative India
Proofread by Gillian Fitzgerald-Kelly
Cover design by Jack Smyth, jacksmyth.co
Cover image © plainpicture/Daniel Allan
Printed by L&C Printing Group, Poland, lcprinting.eu

The paper used in this book comes from the wood pulp of sustainably managed forests.

the arts council an chomhairle ealaíon | funding literature

New Island received financial assistance from The Arts Council (An Chomhairle Ealaíon), Dublin, Ireland.

The author received financial support from The Arts Council in the creation of this work.

New Island Books is a member of Publishing Ireland.

10 9 8 7 6 5 4 3 2 1

For Tomás

Down along the rocky shore
Some make their home,
They live on crispy pancakes
Of yellow-tide foam;
Some in the reeds
Of the black mountain-lake
With frogs for their watch-dogs,
All night awake.

from 'The Fairies: A Child's Song' by William Allingham

Prologue

The blinds are crunched up on top of B's head and her face is to the glass. It is only black outside. She breathes to make the surface and I watch her finger doing loops and lines. She is joined-up writing.

Me and Mum are on the sofa that is soon time to put the sheet on for bedtime. She jigs her knee to say my cuddle is over but I go too heavy on her lap and ha she cannot move. I can stay to ask all questions like one now—what is a fortnight?

Two weeks says Mum. She knows I am asking because of all the talk, a fortnight is not long, a fortnight is as much as is possible. A fortnight is plenty of time to find somewhere else. Mum is holding up two fingers as if I don't know what two weeks is—we have been here for two weeks and that is a fortnight. God only knows why it is called a fortnight.

A week is all the days one after another then is another week. Mum says go and play now while I make the bed, but it is too late to go outside and there is no climbing whatsoever in the house. We must play quietly because Diane who is the woman doesn't like noise. Paul is the man. He has a beard and says Diane is trying to watch the television. It is a joke for just us *Diane is trying to watch the television* but we have to whisper. We are not staying. It is just until we find somewhere and we will find somewhere soon there is nothing to worry about.

The door opens like a shock a bit because it is just us three in the room and nobody comes ever. It is Paul the man with the beard—his eyes are looking around. He lifts his big arm and points at B with a finger. That is rude but Mum doesn't tell him. Mum is watching.

I've told her not to do that, he says in his voice that is not scary it is just an accent. B looks at him and her finger is still.

I'll clean the windows, says Mum and is bright.

She'll break those blinds, says Paul. He swallows something right into his mouth all beard and goes louder a bit. You can't stay here any longer. It's time to go tomorrow.

He is walking away. I am off Mum's knee in a rush and she is following him.

We have nowhere to go, she says in the corridor. There is a door shut and then a long quiet afor Mum is back. Her face is well I never isn't that something.

B is wiping all the writing from the window, with her hand holding her sleeve like it is to put your arm in the coat and hurry up come on please. I'm sorry she says and her lip is if she will cry. She never cries but only because she is older and I will not too when I am her age.

Mum gives her a hug that makes me want a hug as well so I go over to have some for me.

He was coming in to say that anyway. We'll just have to get on with things now. They said two weeks and it's been two weeks. That was only a coincidence.

What is a coincidence?

Part One

December 1988

If the crows call two times I'll kill him. But if they only call once then he lives. Crows don't make birdsong, they speak out and if you listen hard it's either a double or single call they end with. They'll tell me if today is the day. When he comes his engine will be louder than the crows, but I'll listen and I'll know what to do.

The place to stab is in the neck straight away. I'll land on the roof behind the cab. He won't know I'm there, and when he climbs out, he won't have time to look left or right afor I'm on top of him. I free one hand to take the knife from out my teeth. It's foreign from France with a band that stops the blade folding. This is a fighting knife, and is sharp as new because I save it only for real attack. It's not for whittling sticks or carving the spoons that Mum likes.

The crows live in the big grey chestnuts up by the gate. To get to the barn Jerry Drain has to come down past them. He has to slow nearly to a stop to turn here by the garage. His Toyota Dyna used to be a flatbed, but he built a shelter on the back of it with metal sheeting and painted it the same red to the rest. There's melted bubbles at the joins where he's stuck it together. It was a truck and now it's a van so he can steal more and more of our hay. I know his tyre marks in the mud, over and over. Big curvy triangles that always give him away. When we arrived in the summer the barn was full with hay and straw but it is going down and down. Every time I come back from school, I check the barn and there's less. He'll empty it completely and then everything will be gone.

The mud is dry now on my cheeks and my forehead, it cracks when I frown and when I smile. The pine sap sticks it in well, I'm the same colour to everything and all I can smell is green.

It's always easier to see out of a tree than in, you can see but not be seen. To look out I have to move the branches a little, but I'm high up enough that no one would see me even if I put my whole head out.

From here I can see the top of Mum's head when she goes by with the barrow, round the frozen puddles out to the back field. Nobody thinks to look up. Even if they did, they wouldn't catch me. I know all of the tricks. Finn

MacCool was caught when he was hiding in the tree because he was holding the branches still, and the wind was moving the other ones around him. So when the wind blows I sway a bit and move my treetop too.

The crows will hear him afor me. They hop from place to place and nod and croak. You can see the movement of their heads, and their wings out when they land. It's difficult to find their nests, even in the bare branches, but one is there, and another, and then they're everywhere, knots of sticks caught. When you listen you can understand what they want.

I count the calls. They change every time over and back—one for peace and two for death.

The last time he came I was watching and I didn't move. I'll get him if he comes today. I'm on just the right branch, and if the last crow calls two times I'll jump.

The pothole clang of the Dyna. It rattles when he's on the brakes and shakes like thunder on the straight. Jerry Drain. The sun flashes on his windscreen and the crows all call together like shouting at once and I cannot tell how it ends. Now is all engine and the bull bar comes out from the shadows of the chestnuts—he has two fists on the wheel and his mouth down. He's up right below me loud and the engine slows.

I do not know to attack or not, it is the time but I do not know and then it is too late. I can't see him anymore, but he'll be turning, reversing in under the barn, making more to the same tyre tracks. The engine's off now and the crows are calling. Two and two, and four and three, they're saying kill him, kill him, but now they're saying wait.

I climb higher and wedge in. There's bunches of knobs on the branches about. The death blade cuts through the little twiggy stalks of them easy. They're like pine cones but not, they're small and round, heavy little balls with cracks. I collect them up in my lap.

The engine starts and I stick my knife in the trunk. I grip the thin crown of the tree with one hand, and stand up. I'm right out from the top, the cold is all over me prickling through my gansey. The rest of the tree stones have fallen, but I have three or four in my fist and I fling them down at the roaring van. They all hit the top, bouncing in a spray.

Little stones spit out behind his wheels. He's braking, but he hasn't even got as far as the chestnuts. He stops with a jerk, dead opposite the house.

Was I in the wing mirror? The branches are closed above me, but the tree-top sways. I'm swinging high up in the sky though there's no wind. I can see in above the tailgate, all is stuffed with hay. One crow call from the chestnuts, and three small and quiet in reply. I duck down and reach for my knife. My wrist is tense and strong—if the wrist bends the knife won't go in. I open my eyes. The crows said to wait, it was not time to attack. But now it is too late.

I hold my breath and listen. The van door opens and slams shut. The tree is nearly still. Careful, I pull down a branch.

He's not even looking in my direction, he's walking straight across the grass and up to the front door of the house. What on earth does he want? He doesn't even know to go down between the sheds to the kitchen door at the end. The front door is only for patients. It's like he's going to ring the bell—he half reaches for the rope. We don't ring the bell because it makes an awful noise and Mum shouts and is angry. I hope he tries it, it will be a big mistake for him. He steps back though, and forward again. The window panes upstairs rattle when he bangs the knocker down. The back of his head is the same to a clot of blood under the skin of your thumb. His nose might be touching the door his head is so forward.

Mum won't be happy about this. She'll have to slide the big wooden bar into the hole in the wall and then lift it up and out. It's heavy and awkward. The door is either open all day or it's closed and that's that, it's not to be opened. Jerry Drain is standing with his elbows pointing out, his knuckles on his hips and his fingers out flat like two flaps.

When Mum knocks on somewhere she'll come away a few steps and turn, so when the door is opened she'll have her back to it and only spin round at the sound. Jerry Drain doesn't move, he doesn't change his head or step back.

He's waiting there a long time, but he doesn't knock again. The door opens and it's too far away to see the expression on Mum's face but Jerry Drain takes a step back and one hand goes into his pocket. Mum nods her head, and nods her head again. Jerry Drain nods his head, and nods his head again, and then Mum shuts the door.

As he comes away, he's walking slower, his head isn't pushed out anymore, and he's looking at the ground. He climbs into his van and drives away quietly.

These tree branches are so thick together that I can jump off the top and just fall prickly down through, every bit a soft drop until the ground.

The sun has gone now, there's no shadow under the trees. The whole sky is one colour of grey, the house is a lighter grey than the sky but the slates are darker. Light comes out the kitchen window onto the hedge, otherwise the wall and the cloud, the tree trunks, grass, slates, the telegraph line are all just different greys. The spaces between them are no longer there and one thing is becoming another. The crows have stopped calling and the black bars of the gate fuzz. The darkness has come so slowly that I never noticed and now it is almost here. The kitchen window is like an ember in ash. I run towards it afor the dark comes black down.

Today is gone on me already, and nothing done. There's hardly eight decent hours in it.

Too late to go back for another load now, be disturbing them in the dark. No light in the barn anyway. The headlights might do, but it'd be slower going, be wasting time. I'll leave it, I've enough now anyway.

I shouldn't have said anything. That was a mistake. Only ever a waste of time talking to people. But he'd have every bale gone on me. How many times have I come in and he's climbing in on top to them, jumping off them, hiding in behind them. Split bales are as awkward, there's the same work in one of them as ten of the others. Will I go for the barrow? As quick just gathering it up in my arms.

I'd have just had a word in his ear only he takes off at the sight of me.

She never took her eyes from me when I was talking, no expression on her face.

– Well I'm quite sure he's not doing it intentionally.

Well I'm quite sure all the shagging twine is broken, is what I might have told her. A cut-glass accent, is that what they say? You might cut glass with it alright. And the look in her eye could split you in two.

I never saw her up close before.

The Archers come on the wireless at five past seven o'clock. Mum and me keep watch on the kitchen clock as it comes up to seven, and then from about five to I'll hardly look at anything else. Mum hates to miss the start but with me she never will, I make sure every time. It takes ages but it comes round to four past eventually. If Mum turns the knob on the wireless when the red second hand comes round to the twelve and the minute hand clicks forward one big tick to the five, we'll land in the silent bit and can wait for the music to start.

And off it goes. Mum sometimes hums along and does a jerky kind of dance around the table, with one hand held up and the other elbow out like she's dancing with someone not there—or she'll hold her fists held tight and squeezing as if she's playing an accordion. I'm not to make a sound then when the talking starts—if I want to be noisy I can go out in the lane between the sheds or next door to the dining room. I can be anywhere but the kitchen.

At two minutes to seven she asks me did I shut the gate. I remember looking at it open, down through the trees after Jerry Drain had gone.

You forgot the gate.

But outside has changed completely, it isn't there anymore. The window is so dark that there's only the kitchen in it. I can see the dogs curled up in the chair with the cat, the range and the round silver of the lid that's down, the metal spirals of the handle. And the gate is standing open in the dark.

The rush matting on the floor is a square that goes inside itself round and round until the rope line ends in a little squiggle in the centre.

You promised you'd do the gate.

There's something caught squashed in the weaving. It's the colour of the tick we found on Rosemary's leg. She was limping and not wagging her tail but we couldn't find anything wrong with her paw. The pads weren't broken and in the fur between them it wasn't hurting her or anything. It was giving her leg a rub after, that I felt it. She had been limping because the tick was taking all the blood for God knows how long, and the limp was only getting worse. A tick bigger than my thumbnail, the same kind of ridges on it, the same colour to whatever is in the strings of the square of matting by my toe.

Go and do it quickly, before The Archers starts. Run along.

If B was here she'd come with me. When we go for a walk we never take the same route back, because the Devil sees you on your way out and waits by the path for you to return. But B will be double figures next year, and Granny and Grandfather England are paying for the school so she had to go. She comes home only at the weekends now. She gets ten pence pocket money, we have a penny for every year so I only get seven. When I am eight I will have eight pence. All B ever does is save hers. I've never found her treasure box but I will.

If you don't do what you're told before The Archers starts you'll be extremely sorry.

Sometimes we leave the gate open, if there's to be patients. If I say it loudly it might be more true.

I thought we might be having patients.

Don't lie to me, you know full well patients rarely come in the evening and I tell you if they do.

I go to the window and the shapes of the bushes step forward. I can't go out in the dark. There must be clouds in the sky, a layer of clouds that can't be seen, because there's no moon. There's no light at all out there. It's impossible to imagine the daylight in the night-time, it's like thinking about how cold it is in the winter when it's hot in summer, or being hungry after eating a big plate of food. One is always there behind the other, but there's no room for both things at the same time.

Mum puts the torch in front of me. It's black and heavy, there's a big square battery inside it. The battery is blue and attached by a stringy red cable.

If I start crying things will be worse. I can't move—I know what the trees look like in the bar of torchlight. The light is what they like and a torch can be seen from miles in the dark. I know the edges, I see the things that play there, that come closer—then run when the light tries to catch them.

I stay very still and don't look anywhere. I can hear the clock tick and the dogs sleep-breathing. Mum sighs a loud sigh and it is I'm safe. Steps thump and there's a whoosh of air, the front door slams shut.

She's not scared of anything. The door in the next room slams too. I sit at the table to wait for her to come back. It's empty when she's gone.

The knife isn't sharp, the handle and the blade are all made of one bit—STAINLESS STEEL is written. I bring it close, the flashiness disappears when the metal is on the middle of my nose. I look without looking and the reflection is a grey wall. There's little see-through worms on my eyes seeing out. We are falling, I see Mum and B and me falling in the air in front of the wall, falling but soft and never landing, the wall behind is on and on and down. I watch us fall forever.

The weight of the knife on my nose is hurting, I blink and the wall inside the knife is gone. Mum should be back by now. Why is she not back?

If B was here now she would tell me our story. It is always exact to the same and it is like tradition which is when one thing is always as it ever was and that's why it has to stay like that to be true.

Once upon a time, B says every time and it is smiling that all stories are the same. There was a mummy and a daddy and they had two children me and you. B points me and you and I do the pointing at her and me too but the other way. That is what keeps us safe, when it is always the same.

The mummy came from England because she was English and the daddy was from Ireland because he was Irish. Her parents the sir and lady told her never marry an actor or an Irishman and she did both things at once and ran away in a boat across the sea with him. And it turned out that her parents were right all along because the daddy was such a good actor he could never stop acting and nothing was real for him. A rogue is a nice way to put it and he left and there was no money for the rent but she could not go back to her parents.

I am not to ask questions during the story, I can stop B if she forgets bits but questions are not allowed. I can ask after and that is how I know what is a rogue and all of that.

But it also turned out that the mummy's parents were wrong all along too because without the daddy there would not have been the two most beautiful children in the world. B puts up her eyebrows at this bit and shakes her head with a dumb open mouth and I put my hands on my ears, we always do it like that.

We travelled the land and had lots of adventures and we were free of people and free of places and were beholden to no one and belonged nowhere. I can remember that bit so it is good when the story comes true and it is with the tinkers and the bucket and the electric fence and the boy with the hooked nose and all of that.

But it couldn't last forever because nothing does and sometimes when you have children you have to accept that it is better to have a stable house. A stable house sounds like it is for animals and B always says that bit with an old man voice because it is funny and is why we have animals now, Rosemary and Jasmin and all the cats and the two new Jacob sheep. And that is the end of the story, it ends with—and now it is happily ever after and then some. B closes her hands to a prayer and me too and she nods with her eyes shut and I nod with my eyes shut and it is the end of everything. And then at the very very very end B says and now we are here.

Mum is still not back. If my mouth opens I will scream maybe and the kitchen light will fill my mouth. Where is she?

As soon as I begin to pray please God I hear quick footsteps coming. The dogs in the chair stir and settle and Mum looks down at me and I look up at her, so happy she's back. But the fierce eyes she has are blazing and her lips are tightened over her teeth. She had sticking-out teeth when she was small and they put metal braces on them, but she never went back to the dentist. Eventually she cut the wires off herself, but by then her teeth had been pushed in a little too far. When she's cross like this her lips almost disappear.

And not a word of thanks. I ask you for so little, and I still end up doing it all. Who ends up doing *everything*? She thumps her fist into the middle of her chest, twice, three times. Me, that's who. And can you even bring yourself to say thank you?

I say thank you but we both know it's too late. I meant thank you earlier but I forgot to speak anything. She closes her eyes and opens them again.

You're so like your *fucking* father.

She doesn't say this often so it's a special occasion. I don't know what he looks like, but Mum says I look the same to him. I am a handsome boy. He is not coming back and I might as well get used to it. I can only remember him putting a whole big spoon full of Rice Krispies into his mouth and thinking that one day when I was grown up, I'd be able to put a whole big spoon into my mouth. It must have been a long time ago because I have been able to fit a big spoon in my mouth for so long I can't even remember till when. So I'm grown up enough maybe. It must have been Christmas if there was Rice Krispies.

Mum turns on the wireless and The Archers music is halfway through. She doesn't dance today, just sits staring ahead her elbows on the table and her two hands clapped into one big fist. When she dances it makes me laugh and I can sometimes even start a laugh just thinking about it, and I do a skip instead of just walking. When you start skipping sometimes you can't stop. But now she is sad and so am I and it is not good to think of skipping.

When her hands come apart and her face begins to move a little, I go over, lift up her arm and climb up for a cuddle. We listen to the English people talking and she holds me until the end, then she whispers that I have a bony bum and she gives me a kiss on the cheek. We haven't even got the supper on yet and The Archers are even over.

There's going to be soup. The mixer makes an awful noise when it's on button 5 but I keep a finger in one ear and take the other out to put a dishtowel down on the lid over the slow side of the range. It's just okay to sit on with the towel, and my bum and the backs of my thighs are so warm. Mum is feeding in leftover pasta to the mixer into the tube at the top, the wagon-wheel shapes, and pushing old carrots in too.

I take my fingers out of my ears when she turns it off. It's lovely and quiet and Mum smiles at me. Then she looks black. I'd forgotten, she says. You need to listen to me carefully.

I'm listening carefully, but she is a long time not speaking.

Jerry Drain was here earlier.

I don't say that I know, I don't say anything.

You're not to go and play in the barn anymore.

It's our barn. I'm speaking but I can't think how to. It's not fair, maybe it's him who shouldn't be stealing all the hay and straw.

No it's not. The barn belongs to the Pinks, just like the Pinks own this house. It's not ours. Jerry Drain rents the barn the same way he rents the fields at the end. He uses the hay to feed the sheep and the straw for bedding. It belongs to him and when you climb on the bales you break the twine and then it goes to waste.

The mixer is loud on again, but she's still looking at me like there's to be no discussion. It's a lie. I can't believe it. I love playing in the barn. And the eggs, how will I look for eggs? I open and shut my mouth, and do it lots of times for Mum to see. The crunchy cheesy pasta has made a thick paste and the blades are ruggiling then they stop.

I don't break any of them, that's not true. And how can I collect eggs if I can't go in the barn?

Mum goes to the fridge for milk, and pours it in the tube onto the soup paste. It doesn't mix, it runs around the edge, like rain down the window but white.

I'm not saying you mean to, but when you climb on them you break them and you might not even notice. You can go for the eggs, but no climbing, no building things, no jumping off the bales. You know all the things you do.

I'm careful, I only—

The phone rings, it's a thrill sound from everywhere. Mum calls after me to tell me not to, but answering the phone is helpful and I've done it lots of times. It can be people from the Organic Association, or patients, or even news of B. She's not allowed to phone but if she's sick they call and Mum can go and pick her up.

I'm so fast no one can stop me. The floorboards bump and the rug slides. It's rung three times, and I don't let it ring again, I take up the big black handle in the pause. The pause can be the last pause and you can be left waiting for another ring that never comes.

I say hello and wait.

There's just the hum to say it's working. Someone's breathing the other end. I say hello again, because maybe I said it too quickly the first time and they didn't hear. A man speaks, but his voice is like it is a secret.

Do you like Zig and Zag?

Mum is at the door, her eyes are wide. Who is it?

I hold up a hand for her to be quiet, like she does when she's on the phone and I'm asking who it is. I even give her the frown she gives.

Yes.

There's only breathing. He doesn't say more. It's an odd thing to ask maybe, but I love Zig and Zag. Zag is my favourite but I like the name Zig better. So it's difficult to choose. Mum is trying to take the phone and I step away. She's not looking angry, she's saying please give me the phone and I don't know why she'd want to talk about Zig and Zag when it's me who likes them and the question was to me.

Well little Mister Zig and Zag, you have an English bitch witch for a mother. And I'm going to kill her, I'll drown her in the Boyne.

Mum grabs the phone now but my head comes with it.

Then I'll come after you, you son of a witch you—

Mum slams it down. What did he say to you?

I can feel the blood is up into my cheeks. I could never say out loud what the man said, even though it's saying inside me. Mum is her arms around me, but outside the dark is coming in and it is real. The only thing that will be worse is if I tell Mum and she is as frightened as I am frightened.

He said did I like Zig and Zag.

Did he say anything else?

I shake my head and look at the rug where it's scrunched on the floor. I step to the side so Mum can straighten it.

We'll just leave it off the hook now for a while. But you can't answer the phone any more, do you hear me?

You'd never know who was out there. Awful the stories you hear. Just the two of them now with the girl away in that school. The husband was no use, says Mrs Lynch. An actor on the television, ran out and left them at the first sign of success. You'd wonder where she'd get her information, but you'd never doubt her. A fancy English girl with two wild children apparently, but a powerful woman too, well able.

Mrs Lynch gave me the whole low-down on them, she likes to talk that woman.

A mother on her own, and anyone could come in the gate and go down to the house.

She might be well able, but she is surely vulnerable the way she is.

Anything could happen to them and no one would be any the wiser.

January 1989

Mum puts a little container down on the table. It's the same to the size of one of the pots for a camera film when it goes for being developed, but it's see-through like brown glass only it's plastic and has a white cap. It's full nearly to the top, the sugar in it glittering.

Take that over to Mrs Lynch when you have finished your drawing, tell her the same as before—the usual instructions.

Mrs Lynch is different because we know her, but normally when Mum has a patient we're not allowed to see them. They go in the kitchen and if we're in the house we're not even to be downstairs. People can be upset and they need privacy. A lot of them come to Mum when everything else has failed and there's not much hope left. Mum is sad when they have gone and it is horrible to see her face like there is her eyes and they are still. But she is okay really, it's just tiring helping people like that. When they drive up I watch them from behind the curtain upstairs, just enough to see and not moving at all even the tiniest bit.

I saw a bald woman once, her head was yellow and in the sunshine. It was nodding and nodding and her hands going round like rubbing soap on for washing them. She came out of a silver Escort and she was wearing gloves. The gloves made me remember B reading out loud about how witches wear them, and how a *real witch* is always bald. B's voice went funny and low but loud and slow all the same like the priest—*bald as a boiled egg*.

I was away out the drawing-room window and across the fields. It's lucky I don't wash because they can smell clean children best.

I asked Mum why anyone would help a witch and she got cross because she thought I was calling her a witch and she said people have always been scared of powerful women. I said maybe people are only scared because some witches eat children, and she said all that was only make-believe and witches are nearly always good people and people only write silly stories about them to try and say that a witch's power is a bad power when it's actually good. I was still worried though, the bald head kept coming into my thinking and I couldn't stop it. I said even bald witches and Mum knew then that I'd seen the patient so she explained everything.

They put people in a machine like a microwave that uses poison rays to cook things from the inside out. It's a thing called radiation like what there was in Chernobyl, but on purpose. And one of the things that happens is that it makes people's hair fall out. Hair is very strong like Samson, it even keeps growing after you're dead, but the radiation is so bad that it makes the hair fall out of your head. It's worse than dying, the torture they put you through. That's the answer in modern medicine, kill everything and hope that somehow the person survives. If you ask me that's a lot scarier than eating a few children now and again.

It's my job to take the remedy to Mrs Lynch. She is only up the road, you can see the start of her wall from our gate, but I always take my bike anyway. It's more same to a delivery then. My bicycle has three big wheels, it got made years ago for Mrs Lynch's first son who was never going to live to be an adult. He wasn't able to balance properly so this one was put together by Cormac Lovely who lives over in Hill of Down and is fierce capable when he wants to be. It's the size of a proper bike, and goes just as fast. I'm never to say anything to Mrs Lynch about her son that died long ago and I'm not to ask any questions, but she told me all about the bike one day and I didn't say a word.

I'm allowed to go as far as I like on my bike and I can even go all the way to Trim. It's a long way to Trim. It's three miles there and three miles back. After the turn at the end of our road where Jerry Drain's yard is, on the telegraph pole there, there's a green fertiliser bag wrapped round it and a yellow fertiliser bag the same underneath. They've been fixed in with big staples. We're the Royal County. Out on the roads there's signs with paint that are still there for ages, MEATH ARE MAGIC, CORK ARE TRAGIC and LET CORK MAKE THE GIN TO CELBRATE MEATH'S WIN. We are the champions of all Ireland and nobody messes with Mick Lyons, Mrs Lynch says you'd want to be very foolish look at him the wrong way. But Colm O'Rourke is the king man. When he held up the Sam Maguire Cup Mrs Lynch put up both her arms too and shook her fists.

There's a fair uphill, and at the top the big gravel space and the long lane in down to Trimblestown Castle. We bring Rosemary and Jasmin for a long walk to see where they put the mad people in the old days. There's all ivy on the walls and you walk in but there's not much climbing and the fields are inside too. All the time wondering why the mad had a castle and they must have been in dungeons and why the dungeons.

Just at the top of the big hill, there's Foxes' place with the white gateposts, you can see their cattle shed, then it's all downhill but some more a last bit up at the end.

The start of Trim town is a straight where all the same houses are, with new cars in every drive, and trees the same distance apart. It's very smart. Mum says Trim is actually a city because it has a cathedral. But try telling people that, they won't listen to you.

I always spend my pocket money on a box of matches and two penny sweets from Tobins. SuperValu is too big to go into and they have no penny sweets, and Tobins are mean and unfriendly and wouldn't say a word to you and all of that. I read as much of The Dandy and The Beano as I can without touching, and sometimes I even get a page or two open, but they're always watching, waiting for you to touch so they can shout, and they have toys too.

Or sometimes in the summer I go as far as MJs where they have the best 99s in the world. Just watching the machine working. They make their own chocolate sauce. You can tell which are MJs' 99s on Market Street because they are bigger and topping over and everyone has a sideways head eating them and is going slowly on the pavement and licking their fingers too. When the tech comes out, I stand in the doorway of the AIB and watch the big boys go along in groups. One day I'll have a black jacket with a white Y on it and white sleeves. I practise spitting but it goes on my chin.

There'll be no going to Trim today, I have the delivery to make. I put the pot in my pocket so I have both hands to steer. I wouldn't spit in front of Mrs Lynch and I wipe my face. Then I'm pedalling so fast you can't see my feet just a whirr like Billy Whizz and I'm out the gate and at her yard. I go round the back to the brown door there, there's no pebbledash here and a big blue barrel for the rain out of the gutters. I put the bike in behind the barrel hidden a bit.

It's always a long wait after knocking and did she hear me but she always does. You can't get used to Mrs Lynch's face. Below her eyes is dark like it's bruised but they're not bruised because they're always like that. Her eyes are wet as if she's about to cry the whole time and sometimes she does, but she's always smiling too. Her eyebrows are black and grey and pointy like they're holding up her wrinkly forehead. I don't move until she says quickly now, the wind will come in and take all the warmth away. There's a smell of cigarettes and turf smoke and something else in Mrs Lynch's. It's maybe the smell of brown and orange, the colours of the floor. She goes to put turf in the Stanley after the door being open, and I stand beside her. The front of the Stanley is white like a bath and there's lovely chips out of it where the metal below is dark and gleaming. On top there's no lids like in our kitchen, but the hot plate is the same brown kind of grey, it looks dusty and it'd burn you soon as look at you.

A bit of water falls out sometimes onto the metal when the kettle is too full. It turns into tiny balls and are all bouncing and hissing. Sometimes the biggest will be stuck and run and hop from one side to the other, round and a hard pale colour, as if it's solid afor it whittles down and disappears. If I'm on my own in the room, I have time as Mrs Lynch is slow to get about so I might spill a bit by accidentally or spit on the range and watch it explode into tiny skittishing.

You have something for me from your mammy? She calls Mum Mammy or sometimes Mam but it's the same. Your Mam is a great woman, she said, she's worth ten men and they in their boots.

Mum says to say she's sorry it's taken a while.

Mrs Lynch nods, she's been waiting this long time for them sugars. I take the pot from my pocket out and put it on her table. She takes it into the pouch of her apron where she keeps her Majors where no one can find them.

She looks at me like I'm to talk, so I do, though every time I tell her the same. I say that it's like the last time, and she opens her eyes wide a bit to listen and nods along. She's to put a little in the cap, three times a day, and tip it onto the tongue. I say the tongue not your tongue as I can't say your tongue to Mrs Lynch. Her mouth opens as I talk, and I can see the wet of her inside mouth. She makes small huffs from her nose. I've told her all this lots of times but her eyes go all over my face just the same. There can't be anything in the mouth not even water for twenty minutes afor and twenty minutes after, otherwise it won't work at all. If I forget something she stops nodding and stares at me saying nothing. And they're not to be swallowed, they have to sit on the tongue until they dissolve completely. She give me a thumbs-up when I've told her everything. That's how I know I've forgotten nothing, if she doesn't give me the thumbs-up then I still have something to say. I understand because it's like when B tells me our story and there can't be any bits missing otherwise it isn't right.

Sit down and we'll drink tea.

Mrs Lynch is always doing something. There's a pile of potatoes in their skins. She holds the potato up on her fork, and she peels it scraping so only the thinnest of skin comes away the same to the back of a stamp licked. There's no potato lost at all. The naked spud is yellow and clean to a bar of soap. The brown skin rolls on the side plate, all chupped together. It's like the edges of the Boyne that's caught in sticks and branches. She's making a shepherd's pie for himself. Himself is her son that did not die when he was young. I do not know his real-life name and he has a wife with a name I do not know too.

That woman—Mrs Lynch stops and for a moment it looks like she will be sick, she clutches at her soft collar and strokes her neck—that woman he has isn't able to boil an egg. They'll call up on Sunday after Mass and she might not even get out of the car.

Mrs Lynch shakes her head, her clean wet thumb behind the little crook blade of the knife. Her eyes are bad, and there's bits of skin sticking still but I don't say anything to help because she doesn't like it.

The last time I came the table was spread with empty plastic pots and tubs, margarine ones mostly, some Chivers jam buckets. I helped sort them, matching lids to containers and stacking them in, the ones the same size and shape one inside the other, the lids sitting sideways in the top. We found a lid too many and Mrs Lynch scratched her head with one finger.

Mrs Lynch will turn the television on for me though I'm not to tell. The TV is high up in the corner and Mrs Lynch likes it for that little bit of colour and that bit of company. She says the cartoons are a great job and she wouldn't have a word said against my mammy, but where's the harm in a bit of Tom and Jerry, or a bit of Dempsey's Den now and again.

We've no need for saucers when it's just ourselves. The cups have ridges in big diamonds along the outside. Sometimes there's too little tea in the cup and sometimes too much and it even spills because of her eyes, but she gets it right mostly.

It's very dark, and when the milk goes in I watch the dooridawns on the surface of the tea to see if they make shapes that might tell of something coming. Mrs Lynch says not to mind them, and she stirs in sugar so they go away. But I don't mind them one bit. She puts in two sugars and goes for the tray of Mikados from the tin. I won't have more than one to be polite, but she'll take a second one out and put the pack away. It's on the table beside me and that way I can't refuse and I've nothing to do but take it.

The first Mikado I eat in a few goes. I try to remember to put it down between bites as it won't run away anywhere, and it makes it go slower. But as soon as I put it down I'm ready to pick it up again. The second one I leave until I've the tea drunk. I drag the jam with my finger and all in my mouth at once, then I pinch off the eight little marshmallows one by one, up one side and down the other. The marshmallows leave marks on the biscuit. I break it into four corners and let them wait in my mouth into paste to start chewing.

Mrs Lynch watches and she is very interested in the best ways to eat biscuits. I tell her how B likes chocolate Bourbons the best. How she can get the top biscuit off without disturbing the filling on the bottom one. She eats the top bit and then nibbles round the edge so there's no biscuit that doesn't have filling on it. She showed me how to do it. You use your bottom teeth to take off the top—just slowly put the biscuit in until the filling hits the outside of your teeth. Then you bite down, but with as much under as possible to take the most as will come. Mrs Lynch says we'll have to get a pack of Bourbons the next time so I can show her. It's exciting but what if I got it wrong? So I warn her sometimes it doesn't want to come off and you have to turn it over and work it upside down, but this is very rare. Even now and again neither side will unstick and you just have to nibble off all the biscuit as best you can and the filling gets all squashed and messy and chocolate gets wasted and crumbs start happening. Mrs Lynch is nodding and nodding and smiling how you can't be having crumbs, the sweeping brush has to come out then. I say how B's chocolate Bourbons are always perfect. And how she's able to tell the colour of Smarties without looking. The orange ones are easy, but she can do them all. I know she isn't looking because she shuts her eyes really tight, and sometimes we wash the colour off them by soaking them in water and she's still able to tell, that was a yellow one, that was a red one. She's never got a single one wrong. Blue is her favourite, it's the same to my favourite.

Mrs Lynch puts her hand on my shoulder and squeezes it and pats it and says you miss her don't you?

And all tears come out too quickly to stop and Mrs Lynch says it's okay and I'm to cry away and there's no bother and she is tutting and squeezing my shoulder and patting.

When I have finished I say that B comes back at the weekends. I say that because it is what Mum says and we have to be brave and get on with things. We have to get on with things is what Mum says too when it is time to move and we have to hurry now and pack. There's no time for being sad when you have to just get on.

I have the tea and it's perfect only just warm. I like to gulp and glug at it, the way it feels when it's too much and some comes out and runs down each side of my chin. I like wiping it clean with the back of my hand.

Mrs Lynch goes for her purse in the back room and takes out a five-pound note.

Tell her to take it this time, she might be in need of it someday.

I fold it up and put it deep into my pocket. It's sure I'll be sent back with it, so I'll be able to come and see Mrs Lynch again. And I like having the note in my pocket, and finding a secret place to sit to look at it. It's a browny-yellow colour a bit like a used teabag that's dried out. There's the wise monk in furs, I know he's a monk from his bald haircut. Beside him are three animal heads, biting out of big A. On the other side is the thing that's either a stoat or a tiger with no fur. It has a long dangerous tongue the colour of dried blood and its tail is almost like writing. The whole side of it is covered in letters that can't be read, apart from where it says CENTRAL BANK OF IRELAND on the square of white.

It's the same note I bring over and back—I put three little tears in it in the middle top to tell.

The best bit is when you hold it up with the sun behind it you can look through it in the light and there's the beautiful lady of Ireland. If she's not to be found there then the note is counterfeit and it goes to the guards. They don't give you the money for it though, they just keep it. Its name is a watermark and it's always frightening that maybe the lady won't be there and the guards will come for it.

Mrs Lynch comes as far as the gate with me.

That pushbike is still going strong? You put a bit of oil on that chain now and again?

I nod and nod because I'm not allowed ever never to talk about her son.

We look down at the road because there's an engine coming, I know who it is because of the rattle of it far away. It's Jerry Drain's Dyna. When he comes round the corner it's him alright. He lifts his hand off the wheel to say hello but his head is not looking at us. The tailgate is up and it's dark in the back so I can't see what's in there. There's a bump as he goes through a dip and a metal shiver like a baking tray hit off a wooden spoon, but he doesn't slow.

Mrs Lynch's two hands are in the front of her apron, the thumbs out. Outside in the day she looks smaller than inside in her kitchen. She's in slippers and her stockings are creased and twisted above her ankles. Her legs look thin under her housecoat. She's very wide—she's not much taller than me and I think that the length around her middle is more than the length from her head to her feet.

That man never stops, she says. I think she's going to say something else, but she just smiles the way she does. I think of the phone calls, on the phone it was a big man voice, and I bet it is Jerry Drain. But I don't say anything. I can't tell Mrs Lynch—the longer it is the worse it is to talk and it will come right back and be real. Even thinking of it is dangerous. She puts one hand on the wall to be steady, and she won't go in until I go, so I go because I don't want her to stand out in the wind.

Their eyes lifting up at me as I come round the corner, staring at the van, and then their heads turning to follow me. The white rounds of their faces in the wing mirror. What's he doing with Mrs Lynch, I wonder? What will she be filling his head with and finding out from him?

I'll be in Mullingar and out again before lunchtime if I'm lucky. Half a dozen boxes of rods, and 200 foot of square tubing, 2 be 2, 200 by 6 foot is 180 by 3: 30, and the same left again; 3, and the same again; so 34 call it 35. And I have enough of the angle irons, maybe get a few lengths to be on the safe side. Better to be looking at it than looking for it. What else do I need? I have plenty of sheet. I should have written down a list when it was all in front of me, thought I'd save time doing it in my head on the way. What is there I'm forgetting? Nothing.

It's a simple job, there'll be no messing around once I have it in place. There'll be no escaping for them.

Mum is building the wall again, her jumper is tied around her waist and her elbows are bent white. The first wall she built blowed over in the wind and the two Jacobs got out. They went into the vegetable garden and ate everything, all the carrots and purple sprouting, the potatoes were all tramped. Mum chased them with a stick and stood on the wall that was all flattered, shouting at everything. She was in one of her furies and beating her chest with her fist like on a drum, so it was best to stay well away. It's not good to be caught up in it. After she shouts she says sorry. It always feels like the shouting won't stop and it's horrible and then it is like she will never shout again after with a cuddle, and she says we just have to say stop it you silly cow just stop it because she's just being a silly cow but I tried that once and it made things worse. B knows better what to do like go into another room and play puzzles and does this piece go with that piece and all of that and the noise is far away. But when it is everywhere even B can be loud too, saying if you just stop crying she'll stop shouting.

After, Mum's black hair was all over her face and she was saying that nothing she did worked out, and she was too fucking useless even to build a wall that could stand up. Only a few feet of wall, even that was beyond her. How was she supposed to take care of the place if she couldn't even do basic maintenance? And we wouldn't be allowed to stay and where would we go then? We picked up some of the stones. They're the big ones she is building with now, dark grey and flattish, some of them blue to flint, stones a giant could skim. She stopped crying and told us we were good children. She said we were the best children in the world. I was the best boy in the world and B was the best girl.

Sneaking up on her is nearly impossible, she knows every time, and sometimes it's funny and sometimes it's not. As soon as I come from behind the tree she waves at me. The wind is blowing more and her face is covered in hair so I can't see most of it, her chin, her eyes staring out. She has a huge stone down between her knees and she huffs it up, then lets out a noise as she changes her hands under and rolls it up onto the top of the wall. She takes the hair away from her face as she calls out, was she smoking?

Mrs Lynch had a Major with her tea, and the little glass ashtray was nearly full. It's the same one Mum took the ash from the first time to make the remedy with. I nod a few times as I think about it going over.

She'll stop soon, says Mum, like it's half an order and half something she knows.

I take out my fiver that is a five-pound note and tell Mum that Mrs Lynch says she might need it one day. It flaps in the wind and the trees creak. It's their age that makes them creak and moan, just like old people. They might be as old as the house even. Mum says I'm to take the five pounds back to Mrs Lynch tomorrow. If I go now and see if there's eggs, we might fill a box for her and that will give me an excuse to go and visit.

I go to the henhouse first, as I don't like it and to get it out of the way, the smell is very hen when they're all together and it's very noisy like a stomach that might be sick or it might be just a fart that won't come out, but will be happy when it does. But it's a lovely feeling, feeling the eggs. In the barn is better, and where they go mostly. I know where their nests are that they have. You have to watch for rats though, there's rats live in the straw. Alan Stewart's uncle, his father, Paddy Stewart's brother, was playing golf and a rat bit him and in two days he was dead.

I used to climb the bales all the way in the back up into the rusty rafters and touch the ceiling, but now it's all been stolen away by Jerry Drain. He rents the barn the same way he rents the fields at the end and it's his and that's that. But it's not fair, and all the hens had to find new places to lay. That's what stopped them laying, not the winter, there's only been frost a few days, and none of it hard.

B IS BACK. SHE LOOKS STUPID in the navy jacket called a blazer. It has a shield same to an army, yellow and red thread animals sewn on. A grey skirt down to her knee, and socks pulled up tight and shoes with buckles on them. B never used to like shoes. She used to run up Knock Iron barefoot and come down through the woods with the dogs to find the holy well.

She'd pull the thorns out of her toes with her nails pinched and we'd go in the water, the reeds smelled like the lake and there was light-coloured clay that sunk in up to our knees. We brought some home and made pots from it and dried them by the fire, but they cracked. You have to be careful with Lough Derravaragh—three men went fishing in a boat and the water was still, and flat like a pancake, but out of nowhere it tipped them in and the lake froze over quick in a flash and cut their heads off. Then it went straight back to normal, but all three men were without their heads.

B says next year I will be old enough and I will have to go to the school too so I can't say she looks stupid because I will look stupid as well and that will serve me right. It is the condition for living here that we have to go to a proper school. The Pinks who own the house and the fields even and the barn are friends of Granny and Grandfather England but they are not friends of us, and if we want to live here we have to go to the school and that is that. B knows everything and I am not to be scared how it will be good in the long run and there is interesting things too.

She has music classes with a woman called Mrs Booth and her first name is Rosemary like our dog but nobody knows that. B saw *Rosemary Booth* written on the inside cover of one of the music books. She hasn't told anyone though, it would be akin to betraying her confidence. Akin means like. Mrs Booth plays Beatles songs on a piano, and B tells me the words to some of them. I know New Kids on the Snot, they're really called New Kids on the Block but it's a joke in school. I tell B but she says that's not funny. There is U2 and when me and Mum went to Mullingar for flaked maize for the dogs we heard Kylie Minogue in the car. I should be so lucky, lucky, lucky, lucky, I should be so lucky, with my rubber ducky. It was such a stupid song we turned it off. Mum doesn't like music.

We have a tape player. It's in B's room and there's one tape, Elvis Presley the Greatest Hits. It belongs to Dad and B has hidden it so I can't find it. We have to stop because we've listened to it too much and the words have mostly gone off the songs—you can only hear the music really. I know all the words to Hound Dog and I sing it to Rosemary and Jasmin when they feel like it.

B makes her bed even perfect and then sits on the middle to read. Her hair falls forward and she keeps bits in her mouth. I sit on the end and I read too. She says it's not a proper book because it has pictures, even if it is they're small and not even on every page. Her books have no pictures in them at all.

She says I'm only allowed to stay if I stop reading out loud even if I was reading in my head, I wasn't saying the words. It's like sharing a bed afor and B saying I'm snoring when I'm not even asleep. She tells me back the words in my story, so she is right once again. I am to try keeping my mouth closed, and I do that but I can feel my lips breaking free.

It's been hours and hours and it's fine, fine, okay and she puts her bookmark in her book and, you've been patient let's go out and see if the fields are still there and if the river is still alive. She puts a hairband in her hair. She doesn't much ever smile when she looks at you but you can see if it's in her eyes or not.

Out the kitchen door we run at the Jacobs. The two of them are side by side, one cropping and the other head up like a camel. Their necks make them look like goats, but they're not. And they have monster horns—four each not two, horns coming out down and horns curling up.

We don't even get near them because they're trotting away and then running all skittish.

The little bridge over the stream goes to the fields. It is very steep and bare. We were standing on it one time and heard a stone drop out from underneath, the stone glunk in the splash far below. It has to be crossed at a run and then there's the pallets to climb where the barbwire has grown into the trunk of the tree.

We sometimes see the kingfisher from here. You have to be lucky though, and still. Things are invisible when you're making noise and moving. The most ever of a kingfisher is a flash of blue, a blue deeper and brighter than the sky can be and an orange wound below. It flies so fast—only a long flit low to the water, it's one place the next and then gone. It was here I met the badger, head lowed, low in front of him. We looked at each other for ages then both backed away slow.

There's an old tower in the hedge, it has round stone walls covered in ivy and is broken in half our side. We keep plastic bottles covered up under leaves, in a hole in the wall that B says is an alcove. She goes on her tippytoes to reach and her hair goes all hanging down. It's her that puts the stones in. You can tell it's a serious job from her mouth closed with no lips. She takes a long time. They have to be just right, small—they have to fit into the top of the bottle—but big as possible. They're not always easy to find, I hunt for them and B loads them one by one, measuring with her eye when they're exact to halfway. She isn't happy if they're too big and she won't take bits of stick or snail shells. When she's done, and it's heavy enough to cause some damage, she gives me the bottles and I pee in them as much as I can. I add spit, but it would take too long to fill up.

B climbs up first, where the tower has fallen down into ledges like big steps. She reaches down for the bottles and wedges them, gives her hand to help me up. When we join the IRA they won't have to worry about this bit of the country. If the English arrive they won't know what's hit them. We keep guard crouched in the big ivy bushelling, the black berries of it and the white firework buds in among. The leaves are like liver in the fridge but green.

Anyone coming along our road has to be slow because only one car can pass easily and the dangerous corners. We watch the bend in the road up by John Walsh. He's a sergeant in the Food and Clothes Association, all the orders are in Irish and they shout them. He has a grey car but he never comes up this way. There's good puffballs on our side across from his house. They're as big as footballs sometimes, but it's a long way up there, and that's where Jerry Drain has his sheep. Jerry Drain rents that land from the Pinks but these're our fields. Maybe he wants to take them from us, maybe that's what he's after.

All the engines make noises to know them by. Some people get safe passage. Mrs Lynch is hardly out but hers is a blue Fiat with a tinkle in the sound. The son comes to see her in a black Nissan loud and smooth, same a bit to a lawnmower going full blast. There's the tractor belonging to Lyonses, the old New Holland. Anyone else is in for it. We won't attack if Mum's expecting a patient. Otherwise nobody has any business on the road.

Our engine is a diesel and sounds completely different than anything, it can be heard for a long time coming or going. It's a lovely sound, Mum on her way home, like fists going yesss. We have a red Renault 11 D74 GLI. If anyone ever stole the car we'd get it back no problem because of the number plate. That's what it's for.

We wait a long time, when there's a breath of wind we hear it in the leaves, and we gently shake the ivy the same amount it's moving.

A car is coming from beyond John Walsh's, and it's no engine I know. B trusts me on engines and she's looking at me for my nod. I do a slow one. She stands up a little to see when it slows up at the bend.

She gives me the nod back—it's no one we know. We haggle into position, good feet grip on the wall steady. The engine comes towards us down the straight.

We do the best way, stand and aim. Wait just to see the roof—point a finger at the road in front of the bonnet and throw the bottles hard. By the time they land everything has caught up. Mine is the best hit, on the windshield. The car goes swerving, scratching the ditch. B's bottle splits off the roof and there's a quick sea of pee and pebbles soothing.

The car stops but the engine is going. We go low in the big ivy bushes. If we laugh they will shake. My eyes are shut so I can't see, but I can feel B balled up beside me tight packed away.

The engine turns off, the door opens. The hedges are high and thick, there's ways through them in parts but they aren't easy to find and they're even impossible here, nothing can touch us.

We wait and we wait, all waiting. Then the door slams shut and the car fires up and goes away.

B thinks we should go and give Jerry Drain a piece of her mind. She never actually says anything, which is what it really means to give a piece of your mind. It's to tell somebody what you think about them when they have been badly behaved. When B gives them a piece of her mind it just means she's going to go and think it at them. Like sometimes if it's Mum she says we'll give her a piece of our mind and we just go and stand there and stare until Mum is, go away you strange children, stop looking at me like that, and she is laughing but she doesn't know.

At the start of Jerry Drain's sheep he's mended the fences so they can't be jumped and they're harder to climb now. There's a line of barbwire along, but my fist fits between the barbs easy. I help B but she can jump down on her own and I'm in the way.

The river is full, drowning the trees down by the swimplace. They're birch those, the bark is white so there's no mistaking them. Out in the middle the water is moving fast, swirls and it's thick and dark to blackberry jelly. The other side the bank is a bit higher so you can't see beyond. There's cattle over there and they have a muddy place where they come down to drink.

The sound of his whistle comes close and we jump in the ditch under the hedge. There's nettle sting bubbles along the back of my hand and I itch at them looking about for dock leaves. I spit on the stings and keep scratching at them. Between nettle stalks we can see him. The whistle must have come on the wind, because he's a safe distance away—the far end with the sheep. They don't move as he walks among them. Maybe when he comes up close they step a little sideways or run a few paces, but mostly it's as if they haven't noticed him at all. The Jacobs wouldn't put up with him like that. He stops when he sees ragwort, and pulls it right out of the ground. I can see the yellow behind his fist. He walks over until he's at the bank above the river, then he throws it in.

He carries a long black bit of plastic piping down by his side—he's gone to the corner behind the last sheep, a red spray on her fleece. The gate is open, he's rounding them up. He never runs when he herds the sheep. Sometimes he walks a little fast, but his body doesn't move, it's just the legs get quicker. Or sometimes he'll whistle to his black dog and she'll jump up from the grass and trot along low, or he'll lift up the length of piping like he's drawing a sword, but he never hits the dog with it, nor the sheep, though he can wave it like he might.

It's too late to stop B and she's climbing out. She holds out her hand.

Come on, there's no point in cowering.

We walk towards him and it's quiet, only the sound of our legs swishing. A wind from nowhere bends the high hedgerow and pulls a skin all down the river.

Jerry Drain is closing the gate. We're a bit away and he gives a little wave to say he's seen us. We stop in the middle and B says quietly don't wave back. His sheep are on down the road and him behind them, and I think we will go home now but B starts walking again.

She climbs the gate by the hinge because if not you can buckle it over time, and she is always the goody two shoes way to do things. I go up the middle and am down quicker than her, even though she tuts. Jerry Drain is away up the road at the T. The other side there's a stone wall with cement, and that's his yard in behind. I don't know for why the sheep know to go the right way, all hundreds of them. Jerry Drain makes a hi hi and his dog burrows up the hedge and is ahead of the sheep and turning them in. There's a square tower with a top like a castle in there, it even has those teeth of stone for protection for firing arrows. Below is a window with a church arch in it. There's a long shed with a red corrugated iron roof and some is stone walls and some is open. It's where he keeps the sheep when they're not out in the fields.

When we come up to the junction his van comes out. He jumps down to shut his gate and then he's away towards Trim. Let's go have a look around says B and I say what about the dog. I get a sigh that is sad of how stupid I am, it's a sheepdog not a Dobermann and anyway he probably took it with him.

B climbs up and walks along the wall. I'm too scared not to follow and then we're in Jerry Drain's yard with all the smell of sheep. There's an outside pen full with them tight enough packed in, their noses twitch and turn and along by them they breathe but they're trapped all up a bit close. There's warm in the air around them and underneath a slatted floor covered with sheep pooh black greasy like knuckle bones and green a bit if it's been stood on and opened up.

We go straight for the tower, I think there might be some weapons there, a box of guns and ammunition, a sword too. But there's nothing in it at all. An old pallet of cement sacks gone hard, twists of bailer twine hanging off two nails.

There's no way up to the castle bit on top. The ceiling is concrete block and no hole, or trapdoor. I say come on let's go, because my heart is beating.

Outside we see the entrance to the shed and a bit of lane and hedge and B says look, look at that. She's running down the lane the slow way she runs, the wrong direction from how we want to go home. I catch her at the gap in the hedge. There is a caravan behind.

This is where he lives, says B.

I am, ha we know where he goes to sleep but I am scared more too, right close to the caravan and the path where he has walked back and forward to the breeze block under the door to go in and out. He has made a path just with his feet. He is a tinker.

B says he is not a tinker if he always lives here and he doesn't move, and you can live in a caravan and not be a tinker.

I don't like being here, it's like being in the women's changing room in Trim pool with Mum and seeing them taking off their clothes but not meaning to look. And maybe he wants to kill us because he has no house. He wants to take the house for him.

B climbs up the hedge and is looking in the window with both hands like blinkers to see, and I go to be beside her.

I can see a stove, she says. There's a kettle.

I climb up to see too and it's true, there's a bit of curtain instead of a cupboard door, you can see the pile of plates. There's a sleeping bag just under the window, it is open from where Jerry Drain climbed out and you can see the metal of the zip. There's a blanket messy to one side. Mum says an unmade bed is the mark of an unrepentant soul. I don't want to keep looking, I am happy when B jumps down. I get a phlegm from far up at the back top behind my nose and spit it at the window. It is a big one and trickles down. B looks at me but I don't know what she thinks, it is like she will almost smile but because it is all in the eyes you do not know. It is like she might be worried too, or angry. She will say something if I keep looking to her.

There's the sound of the sheep from away, one and then lots, and an engine on the road. B's head goes quick to the side in a listen and when she starts to run we have to be very fast and not be left behind.

February

The porridge sits on the back of the stove all night to be ready. Sometimes, if I look at it for a bit and don't get on with it, it goes into one piece in my bowl. I can lift the edge with the spoon and the whole thing comes away from the china like curd. This makes my throat go inside out and I have to stir the porridge up really fast to turn it into sludge again. Once I turned the bowl over on the table and it was like a jelly coming out of a mould. A dome sitting on the oilcloth, smooth to cheese.

If I don't want porridge I'm welcome to have the oats raw. This takes a lot of chewing, but at least the oats are one thing and the cold milk is another thing. I can drink out of the spoon and then chew the oats full even if they stick in my back teeth. Some husks float in the milk.

There's tokens that can be cut out of the bags of Flahavan's oats when they're empty, it's the same with the buttermilk for making bread, there's tokens on the cartons. When they're washed out and dried on the draining board we take it in turns to cut the dotted line with the scissors. On B's go we leave them until she comes home for her turn. The coupons are all stored together in the bowl with the stamps and the string and one day we'll send away for our rewards.

The window is open for fresh air. There's the crows calling loud and in among them is the creak sound of the front gate opening. It's sure it's Jerry Drain by the way he revs too much and the rattle and clang. He's all guns blazing like he does out on the road but he shouldn't be that fast in here.

Mum comes back from the window with an eyebrow raised, I can tell she's thinking that he's driving too fast. I lift my eyebrow to hers because we both know.

He is always greedy with the hay, rushing to take as much as he can like biscuits without being offered first and not waiting and waiting just taking extra and one in each hand even.

My oats are nearly finished, if I have three more big spoons then I will be done. There will be a few here-and-there bits, but it will be good enough. Maybe Mum will scrape them together in one spoon or maybe I will get away with it.

The door is banging and Jerry Drain is in the kitchen. He has his two hands and arms in front of him, with a fertiliser bag and straw bits and a dead lamb, the black head is twisted on the neck. Jerry Drain is holding it very still. The legs are jumbled and the bony head of it is limp and dolling and the ears are flat. What it has isn't wool and isn't skin, it's bunched up and folded, and covered in sticky like a slug has been.

I've had this fellow under my gansey, he says, but it's worse he's getting not better.

It is the voice from the phone. It is the same big. But then I do not know. I listen and listen but what has he done to the lamb?

Mum has her arms crossed and Jerry Drain steps back, like he might go out the door backwards and fall down the kitchen doorsteps. He doesn't speak at all one bit and then he says, I'm sorry. I've no oven. I don't want to lose him.

It is the voice from the phone but he is pretending not, going all soft and not the same. His eyes don't look at her, it's like when Miss Kelly makes Jason MacGrath say sorry in school and he has to but he looks to the side and he says it quiet. Miss Kelly makes him do it again and properly but Mum doesn't make Jerry Drain.

I went over to Mrs Lynch but she has her Stanley too warm, she told me to come in here, that the Aga would be the right job.

He's looking at Mum now from under his bushy eyebrows.

She said ye wouldn't mind.

Mum doesn't say anything still. She does mind.

But she has the bottom oven open and Jerry Drain is kneeling on the floor and it's just his back and shoulders. He takes his gansey off and puts it in flattering it. The lamb on the floor is trembling all over, and he scoops it up and in.

He stands up straight quick again after and picks up the bag. There's blood on it, straw dropped all over—he grabs it all up, one piece by piece. He wipes at his nose with the back of his hand. There's a bit of straw in his hair, blood on his cheek. His head is looking at the bottom oven, the door wide open like it's not supposed to be. There's a real mess in the kitchen with straw and the bag with muck on it, and the bottom oven is for rice pudding not for lambs. The thing is disgusting and a shiver runs through it, its head on the oven floor still. The dogs are round sniffing and Mum shoos them off.

Why is he trying to cook a lamb?

Mum and him both turn round to me and Mum laughs but Jerry Drain doesn't.

He's not trying to cook it, he's trying to save its life. She puts her fingers in my hair and stirs it about, but she talks to Jerry Drain.

No doubt you've other ewes to see to, this little one probably has a twin …

Now he looks at her with his head up and the full of his face open, and he nods but only by pushing his chin forward, his eyes stay staring at Mum.

You needn't worry, you can leave it with me.

Jerry has his mouth closed tight with a bottom lip out a bit and his eyes won't blink.

Go, says Mum, and maybe it's even that she smiles but Jerry says thanks mam and Mum is kneeling by the bony lamb head then and there's the sound of Jerry Drain's footsteps patting smaller away down the lane.

I go and close the door because Jerry didn't shut it after him and we don't live in a barn. Mum says, fetch me the cushion from the kitchen chair.

I bring it over, the dogs won't be pleased, there's their hairs all over it and they won't be comfy now.

Hurry up, please.

I shut the door, I say. It was left wide open.

Mum takes the cushion and she's whispering now. There, we'll be safe as houses in where it's warm, we'll be right as rain in a little bit.

It was left wide open.

What? Mum's face is sharp in mine and why would she be cross with me out of anyone.

I shut the door.

Oh. She sits back on her heels and then it's like she remembers something and everything is back to usual. Oh well done darling, you're a good boy.

It was left wide open.

But she isn't listening and she doesn't understand. Jerry Drain has got away with leaving the door open, which is bad manners. She's up and saying, come on we'd better get going you'll be late for school, where's your satchel?

I look at the lamb all propped up by the dogs' cushion. One long ear lifts and flicks down like a sick bird wing. It makes me want to not look. The lamb's head goes up a bit, it makes a soft throat scream and flops down.

Don't worry, he'll be absolutely fine—he's happy there with the door open. By the time I'm back from dropping you to school he'll be as right as rain.

In the car she says don't worry again, but I wasn't even thinking about the lamb I was wondering who does Jerry Drain think he is.

Your sister was in an incubator after she was born. It's no different, it can be cold for newborns. They're used to the womb where it's nice and warm. That lamb will be up and running about in no time.

Most of the way to school I am thinking how B is like the lamb, in the bottom oven with straw and that snotty strings of blood. She's not like a baby though, she's like what she's like but with her hair in a long plait and her eyebrows up like sleeping, but smaller enough to go on the dogs' cushion. Her eyes are closed as she's being patient and her hair is wet so the plait is sticking on her cheek.

It is bad to see her like that and I think on her until she climbs out of the oven and stands up straight like she stands. I don't stop the thinking until I have made her be upstairs sitting on her bed reading and she tells me to go away and to stop staring.

I shouldn't have asked. Barging in into their kitchen. Big wide eyes on the young lad. I frightened him, poor gossin. Head low in his shoulders then, like a dog that might bite you if you turn your back on it.

But that lamb wouldn't have made it. Hadn't a hope. Not even able lift its head, let alone stand, and no room left under the lamp: he was a goner. Still might be, the tongue was as cold. And the other one nursing, not a bother on him. Might have another three today or tonight. They'll wait for the night-time. Wait till I'm falling asleep staring at them. You can't take your eyes off them one minute.

I shouldn't have gone into the house the way I did. On her own like that. She certainly wasn't scared though, more like there was some joke being played on me. As if I was carrying a baby in my arms and I didn't know what to do with it. Imagine the worry with a child if a lamb can put the heart across you like that.

I had to ask her or that lamb would have died. And now he'll live. No reason he won't. She seemed to know what she was doing. Handled lambs before. Who knew that fancy English women were able for sheep.

I'll have to bring them up something say thank you. Only what would you bring? What can you walk up to the door with that isn't foolish?

When Miss Kelly says sleep we all have to put our hands one on top of the other flat on the desk. We put our heads on our hands and close our eyes until she says wake up, but she doesn't mind really if we open our eyes as long as we keep our heads on the desks. Sometimes I make little snoring sounds with my eyes wide open and she looks at me and I look at her and she smiles. She has wavy brown hair and glasses and she sits at her desk to eat her orange. She doesn't peel it, she bites into it like an apple. My teeth go funny watching. The only bit she doesn't eat is the little star at the top. She puts her red fingernail underneath and prises it out and she peels the sticker off—she wraps the star bit in the sticker and rolls it in her fingers. Then she pops this little package in the old ink jar on her desk. The ink jar is full of these tiny parcels.

Today we're going to read a story. Miss Kelly shows us the picture on the first page—a big hill with a house to the side of it. And we can read along too, all together. It's very easy because the book is for even the junior infants and I'm already reading as well as Aoife and Yvonne who are sixth class, but I like all our voices at the same time.

At the bottom of the hill was the house.

I put my hand up because it should be at the bottom of a hill was a house, not the hill and the house. Miss Kelly says no that it's okay but it's not, because we don't know what house or what hill. On the wall behind is a picture with all the numbers from 1 to 100 in a grid, they don't look like very much when they're in a square like that but when I think about them in my head one hundred is ever never. Miss Kelly says it's talking about this hill and this house and I say okay but it's not okay. I can't stop thinking about it for the whole story and when we're finished I ask again. She smiles and says it's the house in the story and the hill in the story, not a house or hill. And at the end it makes sense because by then it is the hill and the house, but that doesn't mean it made sense at the start.

We have to write our own stories then while she goes to the other side of the room to do work with fourth, fifth and sixth class and all of that. I write a story about going to the zoo and all the different sounds the animals make. It's very easy because I can think of lots of animals, but I have to keep to animals with noises that I know. I end it with a giraffe because I don't know what sound they make and I thought I did but can't go on, so I just write that I don't know. And that is like a good ending.

Miss Kelly says mine is the best out of everyone's and I try not to be smiling but I can't help the smile all over my face. She reads it out, but it sounds maybe a bit for babies and wasn't good in the end. Then she sits down with just me and puts my story for us both to look at the same time. She tells me that I don't have to use then every time—and she circles all the thens with her red pen—because after one thing happens another thing happens and we don't have to say it we just know. She reads me my story, just to me on my own and so quiet that no one else can hear. She leaves out all the thens and now I understand.

In the car on the way home I'm waiting to tell Mum about my story, I'm waiting for the best time. First, we have to do where she says how was school and I say fine and she asks me did I eat my lunch and I say yes. We say those things if I'm happy or if I'm sad and it makes no difference ever. She sometimes thinks it's funny and sometimes she gives out because it always goes the same. Sometimes she asks me on the way down to St Etchen's and sometimes it's more like until outside Ennis's. But she always asks me while we're still in Killucan, and then we don't say anything usually until Raharney. This time she says, that little lamb was fine, I brought him up to Jerry Drain and he fed straight away. I do not like that she went to him and was there. I know it is him with the bad phone calls. He is dangerous and she does not know. But maybe did she see the unmade bed maybe, and knows he is no good and an unrepentant soul? Did she bring him the lamb right there or just to the yard, and is the spit dry on the window and did she know it was me? I don't say anything because I don't care, she would not know it was me and it is good news for the lamb but I want to say about my story.

I have to wait till we're through the bumpy road on the bog. Westmeath are no good at football and their flag is a dirty red. We're not home until we're back in Meath and past Pratt's and we've taken the last left so we're on our road. So I end up waiting to tell her until then.

All the way though I practise saying it in my mouth—Miss Kelly liked my story and she read it out. Once I've said it then it will be too late not to. It will be already said. But just as I'm taking the last breath Mum says, B has a long weekend coming up. I was thinking we could drive up to Dublin and go to the zoo for a treat.

This is the best news ever never and Mum is laughing because I am dancing sitting down. But then I don't know what's happening because we never go anywhere, and I wrote my story and it has come true. Though I wasn't thinking about me going to the zoo, I wrote that I went to the zoo but I didn't mean me. I was just using I because that's what you do in writing stories.

Does that sound like something you'd like?

I nod and nod and then nod again. I nod and nod until she laughs and she says she thinks it will be fun.

I won't say about my story now, I can't tell Mum about this or even B.

I wrote a story and it came true straight after.

It's too secret. My face is hot. I think of other things. It's not just the zoo. It's Dublin too, they have traffic wardens in

Dublin, they don't have them in Meath, not even in Navan. I've been waiting to find out if the spell works. There's a bubble over the car that means it's completely invisible to traffic wardens. They can look right at it, but not see it so they never give you a ticket. This is practical magic. Mum learnt it from a male witch, he's not a wizard, and he doesn't like to be called either, but male witch is better. There's something to do with pepper in the spell but I don't know how. We'll be able to park right outside the zoo and the traffic wardens won't see us.

When I am finished my homework I go out and Mum is busy digging the garden. I think to say, you're making me cold just looking at you, because she's in a T-shirt and the wind is blowing sickle, but I'm not sure if she'll laugh or it will annoy her. Her face is all red and she has the pickaxe coming down from high.

You're making me cold just looking at you.

What? She throws the pick down.

You're making me cold just looking at you. It annoys her all right.

Maybe if you gave me a hand once in a while you wouldn't feel as cold.

I smile to make her laugh or to make her more annoyed, but she's pulling roots. A worm squirms up and I think of Mrs Lynch's tongue.

Come on, give me a hand—it's springtime, we have to get the ground ready.

B told me spring starts in March.

I can nearly say all the months in order, B taught me. When you get to know them, they all stay, the ones after January and February are a bit tricky but once you're through them it's easy. But don't forget August.

Well not everything she learns at that school is right.

When Mum says *that school* she swings the flat edge of the pick into the ground and tears up a lump, so the *is right* is nearly lost in the thump.

Spring starts on the first day of February. And B should know that, it's St Brigid's Day.

She swings again and dirt jumps up. Don't just stand there and watch, go through that bit and pull out any roots you find. Break up the clods.

Why aren't you doing the wall anymore?

I'm not *not* doing the wall anymore. It's time to dig the garden, so I am digging the garden. I can't be in two places at once.

She can though. Mum can leave her body. She doesn't go too far and there's a silvery thread that connects her to her belly button. If she's lying in bed and she hears something outside she can go and see without moving.

One time it sounded like there were people trying to get in. But she was so exhausted her eyelids were too heavy to open, and it was like she was pinned down. That was when she decided to leave her body where it wanted to stay, there was no need for it actually. She lifted out of herself and up, and let her body sleep.

She went down outside and checked all around the house, floating as close to the ground or as high up as she liked—she could see the slates perfectly in the moonlight and none of them needed repairing, which was good.

Then she was worried that if she woke up when she was away from her body she might not get back into it, but it was so very pleasant that if it wasn't for the silvery thread connecting her belly button to her body's belly button maybe she wouldn't have gone back at all, but she did and slept very deeply until the morning.

It must only be when she sleeps. If she had to dig the garden and build the wall at the same time that's two tiring things at once. But sleeping and floating aren't hard work. So maybe she can do two half things at once and not double.

She's been talking all the time, about how why won't I ever help with the garden, and she is expected to do everything. There's soap working up at the corner of her mouth. I want her to do the wall when she's doing the garden, well why don't I jolly well help with the fucking garden and then maybe she'd have more time for the fucking wall.

I cross away and running. By the time I get to the wall I'm fast enough to jump. A stone slides from the top and Mum shouts behind me. The wind is blowing so I can't hear what she's shouting and the trees creak. The wind is strong that even the grass is flattered and it pushes me forward as I run that will almost make me fly or fall.

There's a big lot of brambles by the stream. I'm careful going in, lifting them with my finger and thumb so the thorns don't get me. The slower I go the easier it is but the twisty pain will always catch you in among the brambles. I pick them out and crouch in a dry hideyhole, well under them all. Thorns is what I think of when I hear the word vicious, and now I think of the word vicious as I look at the thorns. When they come off the bramble sideways they leave a long oblong. The blood from it has dried. It's thick like candle wax nearly. Vicious is one of those words that's impossible to spell, like kitchen.

Mum is at the wall the other side of the field. She's lifting stones up, and pushing and pulling them into place. The sound travels when the wind draws breath—it's not the same to anything else, one stone against another stone.

I am a tree stump in among the briars. Cut down but not dead. And in the spring tiny green shoots will sprout from the side of my head. The ache behind my knee is heat. It is not pain. Among the thin white claw bramble roots I am thicker and I reach down so far and fast that I can't be budged. My eyes water to sap and I do not move.

To be air I am cold, I feel it on my hands and on my cheeks. It is different than the stone cold of my feet—it prickles because it moves in tiny tiny pieces, rising through the bramble bush like a slow wind building. I can travel in it as far as that whitethorn in the middle and hide there and become something else. I will reach the river even and when I am there who knows what shapes I will take.

B's window is up high in the house and it's a cloudy I can't see through. But I know there is the patchwork bedspread. Now she is not here, but when I want to read I go there and sit on the end of the bed. I leave her space in the middle and try not to talk the words out loud. I try not to move my lips and when I make a noise I go away. But as long as I can read and not make a sound I can stay, and she is there beside me. When I don't look it's just the same. I can hear her reading breathing near my ear. If I don't lift my head, she is there. I've tried looking up really fast but she always goes when my eyes move.

The wind blows and in it is a twisted thing, it's the creak sound of the chestnut trees.

But there is something different, the wind has stopped to blow but the tree creak does not stop, it grows.

I look to the noise and for a moment I am not where I am but then it is all real life.

The creak is a huge moan, louder than everything. All of crows rise up into the air out of the turning claws of the trees, skeeting and gulling, all of the every crooked shapes crowded in the sky. There is a scream like a cat fighting but from far away and beside my ears too at once.

The whole chestnut tree above the wall is changing, bigger top falling and the moan is a tear and a crack—as it comes the thump shakes the field like the sieve with flour in it when Mum hits the side with the flat of her hand. The tree was falling and it has fallen.

It has fallen on top of the wall.

I can't see the wall, just the branches.

Mum.

The tree has fallen on the wall. Mum was working on the wall, and the whole tree has fallen on Mum.

I heard the trees creaking, she says. I am sitting in her lap. We have opened both oven doors and we are sitting on the kitchen chair in front. The warmth is coming out onto our legs. I heard the trees creaking and I felt the wind, and I knew it was dangerous so I went in.

I have stopped crying but a shudder goes through like the little ripples after a wave has come in and it is running backwards across the sand away back down to the sea.

You mustn't imagine the worst.

We do Robot. I press her nose and she gives me a kiss, I turn her ear and she gives me a hug, I touch her shoulder and she tickles me under the chin. I never know what each button will do and sometimes she opens her lap and I fall, or sometimes she laughs like a mad woman and it is scary. But this time now she does only nice things.

The Mastermind game has pieces that look like mushrooms from shops but lots of bright colours. One person hides four in a row behind, and the other person has to put a row for guessing at the other end. You have to tell them if they got any right—one little white peg means one right and in the right place and a black peg means one right but in the wrong place. B is the best, she's even better than Mum. Mum says let's try something different. We forget all about the screen and the rows of holes. I shut my eyes really tight and she picks a colour from the box and holds it in her hand behind her back.

I keep my eyes closed, but just lightly, not screwed up. We both concentrate and I have to find out what colour she has in her hand. I start seeing different colours behind my eyes, and I relax and let one become stronger and brighter than the others. Sometimes it shimmers quick in a flash to a whole new colour but I wait until I'm sure. I open my eyes so I don't get confused and I tell her the answer. We get seven right, all in a row, one after the other, but then I begin to get them wrong. It's an orange when I pick red and a black when I pick white. We try a few more but we must have got tired.

Mum puts her arms around me and takes me up for a cuddle again.

You see how we're connected? You didn't need to be scared, you know. I wouldn't let anything happen to me, I know if bad things are coming and I keep myself safe. You will always be safe and you should know that. I'm safe and you're safe, you see. Nothing will hurt us.

Or B?

Or B.

The phone rings and Mum squeezes her arms around me. We do not move. We do not say anything but it is so loud and every time it rings I want to pick up to make it stop—there is just the ringing and it goes on and on. It is like it will never finish.

Mum rocks us until it does in the end.

The sound though is still in thinking like it is still ringing.

Why don't we just leave it off the hook?

What if it was B's school calling to say she needed us?

So why did you not answer?

If it is important they will ring again.

Who is it?

I don't know, darling, it's nobody that matters. Some people are just sick.

Are they looking for a remedy?

No. No, they just want to spread their sickness. You mustn't worry though, nothing will hurt us.

Is it Jerry Drain maybe?

Mum stops rocking me and I can't see her face but I know her expression from what her voice is like.

No, I have told you before. More than once. Jerry Drain is decent.

I want to say how do you know but from how she says it that is that and I must not speak. She does not know better than me, she has not seen his unmade bed. I have seen it and it is the mark of an unrepentant soul. But I cannot warn Mum because then I will be in trouble for being there and all of that. She does not know better than me. It is Jerry Drain and he wants to kill Mum, and me too even after Mum. He wants not just the barn, he wants this house but I cannot say anything, and it is not fair.

March

When I turn my cheek the pillow is cold. It's a school day, but there's no school as we can't get the car past the fallen tree. No one can get in or out. Jerry Drain came to steal hay and had to go away again. He went backwards back up out the gate, the reverse making that whiny noise.

A sound climbs through the window and goes low again. The shush grey outside is a morning blue now, the blue is grey not black. It is the dawn. The machine sound revs, it's coming from out towards the road.

I look out, but there's no view to it and my face goes wet from the window.

I take my brown cap and my blue gansey, it's heavy same to a mat but the cold can't go through. The noise is like a mechanical bee flying, but it juggles and splutters too. It might be something up in the sky. I do my runners good and tight though one of the straps on the left one has lost its stickiness because of burrs. I'll wrap more Sellotape round it when I get a chance.

Outside the sky is sifts of pink and glass blue with a see-through moon. It's a perfect half circle. The invisible side of it is there going on but the edge cutting it in half is straight to a ruler.

There is no noise. Only crows calling and the silence of the cold. Maybe the sound was inside, or it was not real. I try to think of it, but how to remember a sound? I'm wetting my feet making tracks in the white dew grass.

At the bottom of the fallen tree is the whole circle of clean earth ripped up. I never go into the underneath, just stand at the edge and look at the huge bit torn up on its side, little stones stuck in the hairy roots. It's way too big to climb but it's wrong to touch it anyway. It is to be left alone, there's something that shouldn't be seen in that place.

The noise starts huge like a scrambler full throttle. It's coming from behind the tree and there is Jerry Drain's Dyna backed up, the tailgate down. And there is Jerry Drain in among the branches and it's him that's making the noise, there's white and orange in his hands, a chainsaw going. I won't hide to watch him now—that's my tree and he's on our land.

His back is to me and I walk at him slowly.

The saw chatters when he's not cutting and then roars. The bits fall away with stumps like wounds. He isn't turning in my direction at all. He does a big branch and then moves it about with his free hand when it falls, and he divides it into short lengths. The long thin ends he leaves uncut. The flattered wall is easy to see, new logs lying among the stones and sawdust on them like snow.

It'll frighten the life out of him when he turns around and I am right on his shoulder. That'll be the best medicine for him, it might well scare him away, the fact I could have been anyone or anything and he didn't even notice a thing.

He's always going—as soon as he's done one branch he's on to the next. When the saw is stopped but the sound still is, the blade looks like it has a bicycle chain on it, but when it's going it's only a blur that slices clean through the wood at a thousand miles an hour.

It is cold and he is in only a T-shirt. His arms are all red and there's sawdust stuck to his skin. Across his back is *A Mars a day helps you work, rest and play*, and the red writing has a little rip in it. I'm right behind his shoulder now, if he brings his elbow back I'll have to step out of the way. If I had a chainsaw same, I could bring it down on his arm. I could tap him on the shoulder now, give him a heart attack.

The blur of the blade is going through a branch as thick as my leg and it's only taking two seconds a slice. The logs drop, and he traps the branch with his knee to hold it steady but the end comes up—I reach forward to stop it sliding away and falling.

When he looks round at me his eyes don't move at all. He has thick skin on his face and a forward jaw—and his eyebrows aren't chestnut red like his hair, they're orange and low. He doesn't look the least bit surprised. It's like he knew I was beside him all along. He frowns a bit, as if I've annoyed him being there. He waves the clucking blade away from me and speaks up over the sound.

Don't come near me with the saw.

Then he points.

Them small little branches, pull them out of the way. You can make a pile out in the field.

He turns from me and fires the saw again. I take up the bit he's just cut off, it's long and twisty, but it's light. Over the shattered wall, I bring it dragging right out in the middle of the field, until it's halfway between the whitethorn and the stream. I stop and measure with my eyes. One bit is not a pile, it's just a branch lying on its own in the field so I run for another.

After four it starts to look like a pile and after I forget to keep counting. I'm taking them away faster than he's cutting them, because he has to do all into logs. Soon I'll be waiting for him and he won't like that.

The branches rake a path behind me in the grass, and bits break off that I have to go back for. Some make good whippy sticks with a great swish. It's impossible to tell if the whip of it is cutting the air to make the sound, or if it's pulling the air along. I pick up by the thick heaviest end of the big long ones and throw them on top of the pile. Sometimes they fall down but sometimes they go perfect.

The chainsaw chokes and dies with a click. The silence spreads out like a spilled drink on a cloth. Jerry Drain's shoulders fall down and he is tapping at the trigger with his finger. He stares at it for a second then carries it over to the tailgate. Petrol goes in one side and oil the other, the saw this way and that. I keep thinking he's going to look at me but he doesn't. He has maybe forgotten that I am here. He picks up an old plastic bottle of water and drinks. His head is back and drinking so much that he almost empties the whole bottle, then he holds the saw in one hand and yanks the string back elbowed up and it roars. He goes back to the tree and he works again.

When all the branches are cut it doesn't look like a tree anymore. Jerry Drain stands at the bottom of the huge big trunk, it's like a stone column lying crashed down in front of him. His eyes move for once, up and down the length of it. His lips open like a smile but they go down at the same time as they go up. I can see all his teeth.

The bar I have with me is too small, I'll have to go for a longer one. He is talking but he cannot be talking to the tree so he must be talking to me.

Jerry Drain points at all the logs lying on the ground. I'll bring you a little axeen and you can split them for your mother.

I don't tell him I have an axe already, in the back of the garage where it smells dry and of newspapers and cardboard. Mum had a hosepipe running across the lane to the back door. I was worried about breaking it when I saw it, and having to step over it the whole time and be careful. It was fat and round, like it was full of water even when it wasn't maybe.

I saw what had happened afor I did it, I saw it happening like it was already after. I went for the axe and brought it heavy down on the pipe. It cut through, not completely, and a pool of water leaked out. I knew that it was a very bad thing to do but I had to do it.

Mum found it quick enough but I pretended I didn't know anything. Sometimes when you lie you just have to keep lying, there's nothing else to do. She said she knew it was me but she didn't because she stopped speaking after like she was going to speak but then she wasn't, and she didn't be angry so I knew she wasn't sure. She promised I wouldn't be in any trouble then, she just needed to know the truth. That was what was important, and I wouldn't be punished for lying. I knew I had her beat when she tried that. I said it wasn't me, I don't know what happened. She might have magic powers, but she doesn't know everything.

It wasn't good to lie but sometimes you just have to keep to the lie, it gets what it is and there's nothing anyone can do.

I brought the axe to the back of the garage to hide. I keep it under a blanket and I don't often use it because if Mum sees it she might remember the hosepipe.

It was fine when we were working, but he's eyeing me now like I've something else to say to him, like maybe if he keeps staring I'll tell him I'll bring him up a chainsaw as well as a hatchet. There'd be no stopping him then. He'd cut down all the trees.

Did I leave the logs small enough? We might stack them up here at the end of the wall. But there's no reason to – they won't be staying out long so it'd be work for nothing. I'd almost do it to keep busy with him. He done a great job once he got started. Wanted to get ahead so he'd be waiting on me. I would have smiled at him only he'd have known then, that I knew he was racing, and it might have put him off.

I'll kick these few logs towards the others, make a bit of room. Lever the trunk out to one side, then get out of here.

Straight away he's going, darting around, throwing the far logs in towards the others. He's on for piling them. Maybe we'll take a few minutes, stack them properly. No, it's a waste of time. I should be gone from here already, it must be coming up on ten, past it maybe, eleven.

Bring them into the barn, he can split them then, but it'll have to be the next time. I have to get going above in the yard.

Why did I think the short bar would do? I thought to dig out the long one as well, but that would have slowed me. I was optimistic. I'm losing time over it now. Nothing done yet today and the next thing it'll be the afternoon.

I've stopped so he's stopped. He's gone back to staring. Will we keep working or not he wants to know, but he'll only ask with his eyes.

– I'll come back another day and we'll bring these down to the barn. There wouldn't be much point in stacking them here, would there?

Is he mute, maybe? I can see he understands me, but maybe he's not able speak. No, I'd have heard if he was mute. Mrs Lynch never said.

Now we're just standing looking at each other. Neither of us any good to anyone.

What way do I say goodbye? Any other young man I might pet on the head. How do you say goodbye to people? It usually just happens.

– I'm away now, I tell him. And I'm gone.

I won't look back at him, but I know well if I turn round he'll be standing there still.

I wonder what the axe will be like that Jerry Drain is going to bring me. What the blade of it will be, the smooth handle, the feel of the thunk when it sinks into wood—so I go to check my axe in the garage, in behind where the

Pinks have their bikes, where there's space only I can fit in under. I sit down by my axe and spit on the blade and rub it with my thumb so the edge even shines though there's only dark light back here, in below the shelf where the rat poison is, where I am never to go. It's the best place to hide things near where you're never to go.

Mum says even the box that the rat poison is in is too dangerous to touch. The box is open but we don't use horrible things like that which are poisonous for everyone. We don't have rats we have mice and mice are good because there's never rats where there's mice—they're the sign of a clean home really. The poison is too dangerous to let out of the box. If it even touches your hands you might die. That's why it's here on a shelf at the back of the garage behind even the big bikes where no one's to go near it. We can't even get rid of it. Where would you put it that it wouldn't poison? It's best just left where it is, in its box where it can't cause harm to any thing or any one. There's a picture of a rat on the front and the signs for death everywhere on the side. Once I climbed up and held my nose and shined the torch inside. It's a blue colour like the strips of wallpaper in my bedroom. They're coming off at the bottom and at the tops, with bubbles and blisters behind from the bucket of glue that Mum used. There's darker bits and little streams of water run down—my fingertips get wet when I touch it. Where it is dry blue you cannot look at in the light at bedtime because the nightmares come. The poison is exact to the same colour.

❦

I can have an apple instead of brushing my teeth because it's just as good. Some children have parents that make them brush their teeth every night, and some in the morning as well so it's two times. Mum is being funny and it's sure she is lying now when she says, and some parents make their children brush their teeth after every single meal. My forehead feels all stretched from laughing and looking at Mum laughing so I have to shut my eyes and wait until I stop. I know it is a joke really but I am so happy to have the best mum. You see other mums of people, like at school waiting after. And imagine having one of those. Mrs MacGrath even, she is always with red lips and hair that is all enormous and her skin is pink like when you're doing colouring-in. Some people even iron underpants and Mum says she is not joking they really do but she is so much smiling to tell it isn't true and I cannot stop laughing again. An iron is a heavy thing that is for making clothes all flat, it is all hot and steam comes out. Mum says there's one upstairs and I want to see it but she's not sure where it is. We will dig it out and maybe we will iron some clothes even and then we can put them on and be very smart and brush our teeth and say how do you do. I do a walk that is all straight and say how do you do how do you do. But now it is bedtime and we have to get on.

We light a fire in the dining room because my room is directly above and some of that heat goes up. The only really warm room is the kitchen because of the range, and Mum's room a bit over it. We have a story by the fire afor bed, which is my favourite being on Mum's lap for a cuddle but even with a story too. I watch the fire and eat my apple and listen.

B is the best at reading. Mum is good, but B does the voices and we all laugh the most. She reads at the weekends and Mum says it's thanks to Jerry Drain we can get the car out to go and fetch her. She'd been starting to get a bit worried to be completely honest and what would we have done without him. But sometimes things work out when you don't expect it thanks to God and guardian angels and all kinds of other spirits. There's no reason to think spirits are bad when why think anything is bad, spirits are powerful and we have our own spirits inside of us.

But really actually it's thanks to Jerry Drain I have to go to school. Mum even nearly made me go today but she didn't. She made me garden instead. So that was thanks a lot to Jerry Drain too but Mum has found our place and I close my eyes to listen.

Loki is tied up in a cave using the entrails—that's the inside bits, the long guts that are all curled up inside in your tummy—of his son Narvi. I don't take my eyes off the flames at the sound of the book shutting, so the story won't end and Loki might not be alone in the silence. The fire spits and poison drips. I wonder now is the story written about true things because the story made them true, like that's a bit how myth works, Mum says, but listening now I understand with the zoo. I did not make the zoo existis but I made us go and visit and the magic was in the story not in me.

Mum's voice is gentle but it's bedtime. The fire throws out a spark and it lands on the carpet, I lick my fingers and throw it back. It's cold standing away from the fire, the deep walls are black shadow.

It's on my way to bed so I do the same to every night. My finger goes along the left-hand side of the corridor. I start with touching the phone on the window ledge opposite the bathroom, I didn't used to but now I do to stop it ringing. I don't look at the bathroom because the bath is in there, the sliding empty of the tub, and the sink where there was the baby bat alive.

The downstairs loo door is open and the edge of the toilet is showing. I never go in there. The seat is made of wood and there's a curtain that goes under the stairs. It's always dark behind it, even with the light on, and there's something there that gathers up strength if the door is shut. Even with the door open it's restless in behind that curtain. The daytime is no different than the night-time. There's no windows but the curtain moves without being touched. I've seen it happen, and I won't again.

Inside my bed is heavy, and it's very important not to move once you're in and you have the cover up. Even if it tickles your nose, you can't move. There's a new cold bit if you do and even worse a draught of air might come in. I keep my jumper on, but for my legs the hottie needs positioning—between the knees is better than between your ankles, because it curls up in your tummy and when your feet are numb you can't really feel them anyway. It all warms up if you don't move though, you just have to leave an opening for your book and half your head out. My nose drips a bit but everywhere else is snug as a bug in a rug. Mum comes to turn out the bedside light so there's no need even to put out an arm. I leave the book in the bed with me to keep it warm.

Don't forget your prayers. The kiss of Mum, and the bedside lamp is out. But she leaves the door open so the light from the corridor is there. If my eyes are open I look at that light and not at the shapes in the dark.

I close my eyes and am in the fields, how to go about in them without being seen. I see Jerry Drain come walking along the riverbank his body still but his legs moving quickly to head off some sheep, his black dog crouched in the grass and him tapping the length of black pipe he has off the outside of his boot. The sheep have white faces, grass is bright green in their mouths, greener than it looks when it's in the ground. Does water change colour when a camel drinks it, if the water drips out from its mouth is it still clear but shining bright? They come down with the cattle on the other side of the river, in the mud there below the chestnut trees, their ankles in the water because we are flooded.

The phone is ringing, it stops and rings again—water rises over the step and rushes into the kitchen, under the dining room door and going from room to room into all the house.

April

We come in the gate and I see Jerry Drain's van, we have to slow right down to go by. Why's he here?

He's standing over the stones—the wall is gone completely, it's not just smashed, it's gone and he's standing in the gap. What's he doing?

Mum's head is looking at him too. I don't know, darling. She sounds worried, like if whether or not the clocks went forward during the night. He's picking up stones and placing them down.

Oh for goodness' sake, he's fixing the wall! Mum nearly shouts, she shakes her head and speeds up to park. Go in and do your homework she says, and is off across the grass in a straight line. She's cross now, and if she's cross next thing she'll be angry and then he'll really get a taste of his own medicine.

Jerry Drain looks up at her. He's crouching, and then he sits back on a stone as she comes up. Her head is moving, I hope she's using that sharp voice she has for real trouble. He stands up and he scratches behind his head. He points to the corner but with all fingers open.

Mum goes and lifts a big rock so it's standing. He takes a step towards it, and his two arms go out, but then he stops and starts scratching his head again. He squats down and puts his hand on a stone in the centre. I can see the side of Mum's face when he's talking and she's looking at him.

He holds up a finger and she puts her hands on her hips.

He kneels down and starts to move rocks, then he stops and points to one a bit away. She goes and gets it and brings it in her two hands. He takes it with one and wiggles it into place.

Neither of them have looked over at me once. I'm cold just standing and it's boring so I bring in my bag and say hello to the dogs. It's warm in the kitchen and I turn the light on.

I won't do my homework. I'm going to write a story about a stupid man with red hair building a wall, and the wall falling down on his toes and his legs and him not being able to get up from under the pile of rocks.

I start with once upon a time but I get scared and I don't write any more because it's a very violent thing to do. I scrunch up the piece of paper and I go out in front of the shed with the matches and burn it. I smudge up the ashes with my shoe so Mum won't see.

I need to be careful with my new power because who knows what might happen. I stopped with the stories, because it's scary the way they come true.

Miss Kelly asked me to do a story about a mistake and I wrote one where B was left at school. But I was scared so I made sure that she came home okay, and then the next day was Saturday and Mum had a puncture when she went to pick up B. And she changed the wheel but she had another puncture, and what are the chances of that. It is nearly impossible but I knew why and couldn't say. It was my fault. It was even dark when they came home and I was thinking about all the bad things that might have happened and how I wouldn't see them ever again.

So I stopped after that. Miss Kelly was sad and said I can't stop writing. She said she wouldn't make me, because it should only be if I want. I told her I wanted to but I was scared. I couldn't tell her why. I couldn't tell her even though she might know what to do.

Mum has not come in yet, because of the great stretch in the evenings but also because of Jerry Drain. I haven't heard him driving off. He is still outside and so is Mum.

If I go to visit Mrs Lynch I can go out and walk by where the wall is and see what is going on.

They are still there lifting stones and I get ready to say I am going to Mrs Lynch's for when Mum says what are you doing where are you going, like that. But both their backs are to me. They're working one beside the other and a stone falls and there's no fuck or sugar or other bad words or any of them, Mum just laughs. He turns his head and his face is all ruckled with his smile. His eyes are up and down Mum's face and she hides with her hands. I walk by slowly. Maybe I will get by without them seeing me at all and I will leave and they will not know where I am and Mum will be worried. I will be cosy in Mrs Lynch's. I look back when I'm at the gate—through the chestnuts the other side is their heads bent at the ground, searching hands on stones.

They haven't seen me, ha I am gone.

Did she notice him going I wonder, out onto the road.

– Your son …

Her head snaps up, eyes bright as a bird.

– What about him?

Even mentioning the lad is like I'm guilty of something. Will be she angry I saw him go and did nothing?

– He went up the drive … out on the road.

– Yes?

She blinks at me and I don't know what to tell her.

– He can go wherever he pleases.

The way she says it sounds like he has permission for the whole world and any place in it. Wherever he pleases. Like a little lord – if only he wasn't in a tattered old gansey and trousers patched at the knee. I drop my head and go back to the stones,

I should never have said anything. But then she must have realised I was only trying to help. She speaks again and she's softened, there's a kindness to her voice.

– He's probably gone to visit Mrs Lynch, there's no need to worry about him.

Mrs Lynch is away for her map, so I have time to spit on the top of the range. The phlegm goes perfect round into a tight ball and runs bouncing from one side of the hot plate to right at the edge, hops up and turns around and back, sputting smaller until it disappears.

I'm back at my seat by the table afor I hear her breathing in the corridor. I've never been in any other room but the kitchen, the corridor has the same lino carried on through and there's pictures on the walls because I can see the frames. I can hear a cistern sometimes. Her bedroom must be down there as well, and maybe a room from when her sons were little.

She unfolds the map one way and then other ways and even then it's only in half. It folds open another again and it's bigger than the whole table, bits of it drop down the side like a tablecloth. Her grandson got seven honours and that wasn't the end of it, years he was studying in DIT in Dublin and then he went to Australia and away on the oil rigs. All over the place, names you wouldn't have heard of. Africa. South America.

She gets a letter from him when they're sending him someplace else, and we look for it on the map. I help her find it, and I read the name out. Capital cities are underlined and have a black square, and sometimes there's other cities with black circles and I do them too. She has a list in her head of all the places he's been and she gets me to find them. She laughs when it takes me ages—finding Gabon the first time was ages and ages.

Do you know what they call my grandson? she always asks but I don't answer because she likes to say it. They don't call him Cahill like you or I would. They say he's a troubleshooter, did you ever hear that word? A troubleshooter. She knows I know already of course so we are smiling. She chuckles and straightens one knobbly finger in each fist and makes Wild West revolver noises—pischoo pischoo—and says troubleshooter again.

He learnt all his times tables at this table, did all his homework where you're sitting. Right up to the Leaving. His mother might be the high-and-mighty intellect, but any learning he did he did here in this kitchen.

I have my finger on Mexico, it was easy to find. The World Cup was in Mexico ages and ages ago, and I remember the fat little man with the moustache and the witch's hat. I read out the capital, Mexico City. There's other cities but I don't know how to say them at all so I don't try.

Is that the only one marked? She has a magnifying glass, and she gets so close to the page I think she's going to kiss it.

Look at this one, what's the name of this one? I try to say it, there's a jar near the end so that bit's okay and it starts with a G and the ala in the middle is very confusing at once. I say something twisty and definitely wrong. Mrs Lynch wheezes.

Listen after I say it. Her voice goes a bit funny—Guadalajara. I try. She says it again, *Guadalajara*. We do it until she says, that's it. I keep saying it in my head after.

Quick in a flash I remember what I wanted to ask. I'd forgotten because as soon as I came in she was holding up her letter and it was that to think about. Mrs Lynch's Fiat wasn't in the yard, and I thought maybe she wasn't there, though it wasn't her day for going into Trim for the shop and it wasn't Sunday.

Where's your car? I say.

She doesn't say anything. Folding the map back up is a big process. And sometimes Mrs Lynch takes time to talk, you think maybe she hasn't heard but she has, she just doesn't answer straight away.

The mentality of a toddler, says Mrs Lynch. She said that in my own kitchen standing there, her backside on the bar of my range.

Mrs Lynch looks at the silvery bar of the Stanley with disgust and half like she's frightened, as if her son's wife might still be there. I don't know her name because Mrs Lynch never says it, but it's sure who it is when she says *she* like that. Her lip comes out at the bottom and she stubs her chin forward.

The mentality of a toddler. Those are some big words now. As if I wasn't even in the room. Imagine saying that! Not even looking at me she said it. Oh, she had all her plans laid out, she was going to come and pick me up for Mass on Sunday and Michael would bring me for the shop whenever I felt like it. I says to her, I have no need for you to come and take me to Mass, I have wonderful people just across the road will bring me wherever I want, whenever I want—I have a great young lad who calls into me nearly every day, I haven't any need for the likes of you. I said, you may steal the car out from under me, but you won't come and fetch me for Mass.

Oh, they'll miss me alright, there'll be questions asked then. It's not just me she'll have to answer to. Keeping me out of the church is fine by me.

Mrs Lynch has her rosary beads out of her apron pouch. She holds them up like a pirate with a fist of jewels then stores them away again.

But what'll be said when it's known that Michael Lynch's wife has taken his mother's car from her and she's not able to go even into Mass, and she has her husband running in and out to the shops, and him with more than enough out every day with the council.

Mrs Lynch wipes her mouth with her handkerchief.

She got up from the table, walked over there and leant herself back up against the bar of the range. Mrs Lynch's Eurovision tea towel with Celine Dion on it is hanging there now as usual and I wonder did the son's wife put her backside on Celine Dion's face.

And she called across the room, Michael she says, with that accent she puts on, Michael your mother has the mentality of a toddler. As if I wasn't worth even talking to and I'd disappeared from my own kitchen. If I live to be two hundred I won't forget it.

She had him castrated, did I ever tell you that? She had him castrated like you would a bullock and his best years ahead of him. My only grandson is gone away from me, my poor boy is waiting till I can come to him, and Michael, the only one left to me, isn't better than a rug for that … to wipe her feet on.

Mrs Lynch's eyes are full of tears, but she wipes them away.

And now she's taken my car from me. She won't be rid of me that easy. She'd throw rat poison in my tea if she had half the chance. I know by the look of her.

I think Mrs Lynch will spit by the way she makes her face, but she doesn't, she goes for the kettle, patting the air above it once or twice to find the handle.

I better hurry the tea a bit because Mum will be very worried where I am now, I am even worried the way she is worried.

Jerry Drain's van is gone and at the wall is empty. I shut the gate because no one has shut the gate and if you want something done you just have to do it yourself, it's like picking up after everybody all the fucking time.

Hello you, says Mum in a smile.

I think about the blinks I am making, she is not angry where have you been and all of that. I say slow and heavy because it means something.

I was over in Mrs Lynch's.

Oh that's nice, darling.

I could have been kidnapped. I was worried because she was worried but she doesn't care, she didn't even notice.

Has she still got enough of her remedy? Was she smoking?

I feel like filling up with tears but it is more of a blushing in my face. I won't tell her the answers. But she hasn't even waited to know she is just busy at the sink and we should really eat, I'm sorry it's so late, how did homework go?

I know something bad so I say it. What's castrated?

She turns and her hands and arms are wet. She's shaking them out and drying them on the towel.

Where did you hear that word?

I lift my shoulders because I know and she doesn't.

It's when you remove an animal's testicles.

What are testicles?

The balls under your willy—was Mrs Lynch talking to you about that?

I explain that that's what Michael Lynch's wife did to him. I don't want to keep it a secret because it's too scary a bit. Mum tries not to smile, but she screams out laughter instead and I don't know why, because it is worse than anything and it is the funny-lest thing ever and horrible. I ask is it true, because maybe Mum is laughing because it's not true. Mum says yes and no, she reaches for my head but I'm away angry and I can't stand it anymore.

I go next door and take a sheet of paper from the pile under the table where the box with the scalpel is and where we're not allowed and have to ask permission because it's not scrap paper. I don't know what I will write, I just take the page and cup my hand round it like Tracy at school does so no one can know. It's not even a story, I just write that Jerry Drain goes away. I don't want to hurt him even if he wants to hurt us and Mum does not even know. It is Mum who doesn't care about me even if he is a thief and a killer and maybe a tinker. I can hurt him if I want to and he deserves it for lying about me breaking the twine so he can steal. And when the phone rings next time I will answer and I will tell him I know what he is up to.

But now I just write that and no more and it is enough. I write it again underneath in my neatest clearest writing so there are no mistakes.

Jerry Drain goes away.

May

In the evening the itch begins. I don't tell Mum because there's only one cure for worms—no sugar. I like eating sugar straight out of the bag. She has it for the remedies and I dig in a spoon sometimes when she's not in the kitchen. A whole pudding spoon all at once, even that's not too much sugar for me though the taste of it is so full in your mouth there can't be any more. Worms are bad but they're a lot better than no sugar for two weeks. It's just a matter of scratching when they itch. I have to do it without Mum noticing—if I'm in the kitchen I go do it in the next room to have a proper go.

It's one of the good reasons for having long nails even if sometimes they break and get annoying, and tear in straight lines down till there's blood. I get my finger right in where the itch is. My nail comes out that yellowy colour and even brown but it cures the itch and good times I'll have a worm or even two caught under. If they're not in half and dead they squirm blind white looking to hide, they don't like being out in the light. I cut them in two along the edge of my nail, roll up the pieces and feed them to the dogs. I itch until it hurts but I can never get it to go away completely.

Jerry Drain is gone away. Every day first thing when I come home I say that I am going to look for eggs and check the barn. But the bales are there exact to the same to yesterday in my head. Mum says I am fond of omelettes and egg in a cup but I am patrolling because I have won back the barn. The tracks of his tyres are gone and it's like he never was here. It's in my memory but far back like when we lived in other places, or when B was not away.

I have heard his engine once or twice on the road maybe but I am not sure, I have not seen the red of his Dyna or heard the clang when he goes too fast. The chestnuts' leaves are green and cloudy on the trees that you can't see the crows, only hear the crow noise. The leaves are so green it would hurt your eyes. There're just enormous big white flowers way out of reach standing up on some, and sticky buds in my fingers too sometimes when I can get at them. They crush open and I stick them to my face as many as I can. I do a line above my eyebrows or break them off with the bit of twig they're on and put them behind my ears like with the pencils in the hardware in Trim behind the ear so you can just take it out when you need it and lick your lips. I can stick my fingers together and I can stick my fingers to my cheeks. Mum gets the cloth at me when she can catch me and I have to really struggle and fight to get away. You have to be careful near the kitchen sink.

I look checking, but it is safe, Mum's busy preparing to do a remedy so the whole table is clear.

What's the medicine for?

Orf.

What's orf? The pain is going and the itch is coming back, it's almost impossible not to scratch it. I squeeze and step.

Orf is a disease sheep get, it's nasty—look, here it is.

The orf is in a yoghurt pot in her hand. It's lots of a dreadful looking scab, slimy yellow pus bubbles like it's just been picked, dry at the edges.

Do the Jacobs have orf?

No, the sheep up in the fields.

Jerry Drain's sheep?

Mum nods and doesn't look at me though I stare at her with my eyebrows up like she does when she's waiting for an answer.

I thought he went away?

Mum smiles same to if I've said something that is a joke.

What made you think that? She's not listening really, she's concentrating. She picks the orf out and stuffs the crusty bit, folding it to go into one of her long glass tubes. You can't put the tubes down because they are rounded at the bottom. I think of the feeling of a scab between my teeth when I bite on it—my lips press my mouth shut tight.

Everything is going fast at once around and my palms are hot and even they are wet when I touch them. The danger is back. He has stopped with the barn, but he has not gone away.

But I haven't seen him for ages and ages.

Just because you don't see somebody it doesn't mean that they're not there.

Did you see him?

Mum fills the tube with water at the sink. Her back's to me but she's doing her voice that's like she's telling me what things are.

Well obviously, yes, he came to see me about this. Orf is a bugger to get rid of, so I'm glad we have a chance to help him finally. We gave him half the logs for the tree, but he was being kind helping to build the wall—there was no need for it.

Jerry Drain does not look kind. I know not to say it because I am never believed but it's sure he is planning and scheming, the way I am helpful when I want something. How come Mum can tell with me and not with him? She does not say to him, why are you being helpful, what are you after? All I want is maybe another cat's tongue and he wants to kill us maybe.

Some people don't look kind, but that doesn't mean they aren't. Anyway, as I said I'm glad we're in a position to help him—not that I'd wish orf on anyone, but at least now we're not in his debt.

What's wrong with being in people's debt?

She places her elbow on a tea towel and holds the tube in her fist. Her eyebrows go down at me.

I don't know why you're in the mood to be disagreeable, be quiet now I'm busy. She brings her fist down onto the leather book on the table. It makes a soft pock and her arm does a flex sound as it goes back up to her shoulder.

She does it at a speed between fast and slow—she closes her eyes and begins to count. Pock, one, flex, pock, two flex, pock three flex, pock four flex, pock five and on—I count along with in my head to not disturb her, but it gets boring after one hundred so I close my eyes too and listen to the leather tap and the flex of her arm going on underneath where she murmurs the numbers. Debt sounds like something to do with swimming but not good swimming, more like something to do with drowning.

I wrote that Jerry Drain went away, and he did. But I didn't write that he wouldn't come back. He is not stupid maybe. And he is back. The worms are at me.

I go to the other room get at them properly but leave the door ajar so I can hear the numbers if I listen. When is a door not a door?

There's blood on my finger so I've itched too much. Mum's up in the seven hundreds nearly at the end of the first one. I go in for the finish bit.

I wait for it and wait for it like a bottle filling up with water from the tap and then—one thousand. It has to be exactly one thousand. She comes to a rest on the leather book and rubs up and down her arm.

All the water in the tube has gone yellowy, dark like in bog ditches, and there's bits floating from all the shaking like a pooh coming to pieces when it's been in the water too long. She takes the cork out, and draws up some of the yellow water in her little pipette. A tiny bit of scab goes too.

I hold out a tube with new water, and she drops one single drop in, then she gives me a cork so I can put it in the top. The drop spreads out and there's the brown speck of scab that came with it but otherwise the water's almost clear. She squeezes out the rest of the pipette in the sink and pours the old tube in. Most of the orf goes rinsed down the plughole, but some is left caught in the glimmer metal bit.

Mum takes the new tube from me. She nods instead of thank you but I know what she means. Sitting down, she moves her head from side to side. She'll go all the way to one thousand again, one after another after another, staring ahead with her eyes shut, concentrating on the count.

This time I stay all the way to one thousand but I do not listen to the numbers much—I creep around the table and Mum in circles and nobody can hear me not even me and sometimes the itch makes my knees go high like I am stepping over long grass or thorns and thickets. I cannot use my hands to scratch, my fingers are all bunched tips with the quiet of the creeping circle.

When it is one thousand and Mum has finished blinking and rubbing her eyes we do the same again, just one drop into the water. I look for the speck of scab but I don't see it. The thousand shakes has taken the tiny yellow colour out.

She opens her notepad and draws two little lines because she's done it twice now. She keeps a tally like prisoners in jail with bars in the high-up windows. On the stone walls—four down marks and the fifth one goes across to make five. Two groups side by side are ten and then she goes down a line, when she's done ten lines that's one hundred. She won't do them all tonight, maybe we'll do five and then she'll say that's enough and it's time to get the kettle on for a hottie.

The water is completely clear now. But the essence is being drawn out of it, and you can't see the essence of a thing. The purer something is the less you can see, it goes more invisible the stronger it becomes. It already looks gone and she's only done two, by the time she's done one hundred, the essence of the orf will be so strong that it will cure the sheep with no problem.

She has closed her eyes now and I do too. I listen to the numbers one after the other and the steady sound of Mum's fist as it taps on the leather book on the table. Every time is a tiny bit of power growing.

June

B is walking past my bed. She is going quietly to not wake me and she opens the door to Mum's room slowly. The handle clinks round so it doesn't make the loud scrunchy sound. When she shuts the door behind her I jump out to follow.

The curtains in Mum's room are thicker so it's darker, but she's putting on her side light and the lovely shady orange. Hello my little darlings, how nice to see you, quickly now.

I climb onto the bed the other side, and in where she's holding the covers up, snuggling into the big warmth. Mum is cosy and I can feel B's arm but I move so my arm isn't bothering her and all of that.

We lie with our heads in by Mum's chin getting comfy, one under each arm. Once we're settled no one can move even their legs or cold air can get in, so we all cuddle in close and it's the best. We're all very quiet like mice.

I can hear Mum's heartbeat, and listen to her breathing. It goes slower and deeper and to make sure Mum doesn't sleep I pat her tummy.

Shush, don't do that I need to pee.

Can we have a story please?

B always is sure to say please, she does it on purpose. All how annoying she is I remember now. I slide my arm up under and throw hers off. Mum hisses because of the cold air. B doesn't put her arm back and I feel sad.

What would you like a story about? Maybe Barry and Jane?

B's arm comes back. This is the best—we never get stories about Barry and Jane, only in the holidays and in long car journeys. Barry and Jane are brother and sister and have adventures together.

Did I tell you about the time Jane went away to boarding school?

We shake our heads, the covers rubbing our noses. Mum starts to explain that Barry wasn't old enough so he stayed behind, but one holiday Jane came home. They were very nice to each other because, although they pretended otherwise, they missed each other very much.

We laugh because we know that Barry and Jane are like us and Mum talks to us and makes jokes about them and what she's really doing is making jokes about us. It's very clever but at the same time Barry and Jane aren't like us at all, so it's not about us really.

We don't get up for ages, and Mum says it's time to shake a leg lots of times. We have a guest for lunch today too, so we have to get ready.

Who's coming?

And no barricades please you two, do you hear me?

Who's coming? Who is it? Who is it? I do the questions and B goes to open the curtains—then we see how much morning it is, the whole room is daytime.

B says, you know she won't tell us so there's no point in asking. The best thing you can do is be patient.

Mum goes straight out to the garden after breakfast and B puts a finger to her lips until it is sure we're just us two. She stands up and puts her hands behind her back.

As you're no doubt aware it's Mum's birthday soon, she's going to be thirty years of age. This requires a certain degree of celebration. What ideas have you had for an appropriate gift?

B always says words to make me not know, but it's Mum's birthday soon, that's the important thing.

Do you want me to fetch your colouring book and you can do one page very neatly? We can cut it out and stick it to some cardboard. Or will you draw a picture?

I did colouring-in last year and B was cross when I went over the lines even though it wasn't her page and it seems a bit like for babies.

I'll draw a picture.

Okay, go and find your pencils and I'll get you some paper.

What have you done for her?

It's a surprise, B says from next door. She's going to the paper pile under the dining room table that we're not allowed to touch. She won't tell me so there's no point in asking. I have to be patient. It's exciting taking sheets of paper clean both sides and not scrap. Hers will be much better than mine. Maybe she'll have used some of the flat flowers in her flower press and have done something really pretty.

She puts two sheets on the table so I have a spare if I mess up.

Make a proper effort and do something good. I'll be back to check.

I take the blue pencil for the sea with big waves, I just do the lines, I'll colour them in after, and the brown pencil for a boat coming out. I make sure to do the planks at the side to show it's a proper boat. I do sails with red and big masts to hold them. I use green in the sea as well as light blue and dark blue. It looks really good even if a bit liney. I put grey and some of purple then and black because it can be a storm and exciting too.

I have to lay the table. There's one guest so we'll be four and there's no need to do it in the dining room, we'll just eat at the kitchen table as usual. B has peeled the potatoes and they're yellow under water. I hear an engine and it might be the guest, but out the window is Jerry Drain—maybe he's come to cut up the rest of the tree.

Mum scoops the peelings into the hen bucket. She takes the J-cloth from the sink and wipes the table all wiping, tells me again for the last time to get the knives and forks.

Jerry Drain is at the kitchen door now, bending his head to one side. He should be at the front door if he wants something. I don't know why Mum has the kitchen door open when we should keep it shut. It's not nice him looking up and down into our house. I stare at him right in the eye with go away in my head and he stares back. I turn to Mum because she hasn't seen him so she'll ask what he wants.

But Mum just tells him come in, come in.

I don't want him to come in, but he's in the kitchen now. And it is real and happening.

This is Gearóid, says Mum.

Hi chilren, he says—he doesn't even know how to say children properly—and he gives us a wave, his whole forearm moving. He has a big green bottle tucked under his arm.

He puts a blue and red striped plastic bag on the table, the sides of it are all sticking to what's inside—raw meat, lamb chops by the look of it. A whole bag full of lamb chops. The top where he was holding it twists slowly open and it's lamb alright, cutlets and those bigger ones with the ring of bone in them. It would take me two hands to lift the bag.

Hello, says B and it turns out Jerry Drain is the guest.

The big bottle is 7up, fat and bright and green. Mum will be angry about that, it's full of sugar, but it sounds like she's lying by the smile on her face. B has seen the 7up too, we both take a step towards it. The guy is on the label, it's cool to be clear. The bottle is right full up to the neck and that plastic bit under the cap is unbroken. Maybe it isn't for us, maybe it's his and the lamb chops too. He's lying somehow. I know that much.

Say hello, don't be shy.

She's wrong, I'm not shy I just don't like liars. She's even saying he's a bit shy aren't you darling, sometimes, a bit. I get too angry not to speak.

I thought you were called Jerry Drain, I say.

Gearóid Ó Direáin is my name. People up here in Meath call me Jerry Drain because they can't speak Irish.

I know John Walsh can speak Irish, all the commands in the FCA are in Irish and you have to be able to speak it to join. Miss Kelly at school speaks Irish too, and we're learning. So I tell him people in Meath can speak Irish. I can speak Irish. I use an easy one, to make sure I'm right. Tiger is *tíogar*, I say.

He nods like I'm wrong, lifting his chin up instead of dipping it down.

That's only shop-bought Irish, he says. They have words for things that don't even exist. You won't learn Irish in there in St Etchen's.

Does he know about Miss Kelly and the numbers one to one hundred on the wall? About how she eats an orange like an apple too? He's smiling like he's made a joke.

He's looking different, and it's not just because he's close up and in our kitchen. His hair is brushed, he's combed it even, so it doesn't look natural. It's all scraped over to one side and there's a straight parting, it doesn't want to stay down all the same. It makes his head look dishonest.

He mustn't think I know very much. There's a gaeltacht out towards Athboy where everyone speaks Irish, all the signs are in Irish only. I've even been through it.

What about Ráth Chairn? I tell him. They all speak Irish there.

He opens his mouth and closes it again. Arra, he says, then doesn't say anything else.

Arra? Maybe it's Irish for I'm wrong.

Mum picks up the 7up bottle. She lifts her eyebrows as if there's something funny and gets glasses, like we're being naughty and she's being naughty with us, and she fills them both right to the top.

She takes the big pan and starts lifting chops out of the bag. The fizziness has left my mouth numb but swallowed in 7up taste. I tried to drink half and then leave the other half for sipping, but I couldn't stop, the sips turned into big glugs and then it was all gone. My glass has only drops left and I drip them onto my tongue. The bottle is still mostly full. I look at the line, where it goes dark green and thick and all the tastiness is.

I stare at Mum until she sees me, and point to the 7up but I don't say anything. I'm not asking for more, just making it look like it. She'll never let us have another glass unless she's a liar too.

Ask Gearóid.

I don't know why she's saying Gearóid like that when she always used to call him Jerry Drain. The way she says it is not the same to how he said it. I won't ask him anything.

It's for ye two chilren, drink it up.

I give Mum a look like she knows what she's done, but I go for the bottle straight away. B was saving hers, same to all the time, so she's hurrying to finish it now. I have trouble even with two hands with the bottle and Jerry Drain is watching me. I do it without spilling but it takes a long time and B has her glass empty. She takes the bottle off me and fills her glass up and I haven't even started. The bubbles hurt so I have to stop for a breath.

Slow down you two! Mum has a weird laugh that's not her laugh.

She turns the chops and I look at the table, I won't look at him. B says nothing and he says nothing and we all sit there saying nothing, and the nothing is a big thing. Jerry Drain picks up the bottle of 7up and he fills our glasses. He winks at B and she smiles because she's stupid. I won't drink it, I've had enough sweet drinks. The bubbles come up in little lines of dots. I have a last bit and then more. He is smiling at me but I am looking at the table and the wipemarks on the oilcloth. And then I have to burp and I lean down to do it under.

How did the orf work out? Mum says in the more silence.

Jerry Drain's face is different, like he can't believe his eyes.

Gone completely.

It is he needs to say more but isn't saying anything. Then he goes, I've never seen anything like it. He shakes his head remembering and Mum is trying not to smile and talking in a rush about how well animals respond and how they are not as complicated as humans and all of that. I whisper to B that it was one-hundred-strength remedy because she was not here and she doesn't know, so I will tell her.

The chops are so many of them and we only ever have two, but there's still a pile in the dish in the middle and Jerry Drain says put more on.

Mum does and you can hear them frying and you can smell the smell of them. It's slow with the knife and fork and some of the rubbery cutting takes ages.

Will we eat with our hands maybe, says Jerry and he picks up a chop in his fingers. I look at Mum and she's smiling again and I grab a chop and I eat until I can't eat any more—the round pure meat bits first and then the crispy fatty down bits. There's meat stuck in my teeth and I haven't even eaten the potatoes. I forgot to put the butter on and if I do it now it won't melt. I chew the bone and nail out the bits stuck in my teeth. Jerry lowers more chops on my plate. What do you say says Mum and I make my lips move so I've said it but I don't say it because I know only I can hear it—thank you.

Eat up your potatoes—knife and fork!—and she's angry that I haven't said thank you but hiding it in her voice, even if I actually did, and it's just because the half spuds go quicker with your hands.

And your purple sprouting.

I go through the purple sprouting for caterpillars just in case. Mum is eyes at me to stop because she checks them carefully when she picks them and anyway once they're boiled they're perfectly fine to eat. But I don't stop because finding one as you're eating them is horrible and I have found half ones even. It's not a joke. What's worse than finding a worm in your apple—half a worm. It's true.

I eat everything so I can go back to the chops. But the pile in the middle gets bigger instead of smaller and I slow down because there's more chops than I can eat. I drink another glass of 7up to try and get rid of the dryness and fullness but it doesn't help. I can't eat any more.

Mum and Jerry talk sometimes and sometimes she tries to make us talk. She asks us questions as if she doesn't know the answers even though she does. B talks and is showing off by being polite. Mum and Jerry have tea and Jerry asks does B drink tea and she says no. He must be stupid—B is ten only and that's not that grown up even nearly. Mum doesn't know I drink tea in Mrs Lynch's.

They sip their mugs and it's good because there's nothing after and then he'll go away and leave us in peace. Jerry Drain says there's a man he does some welding for over in Collinstown has a little boat that he keeps on Lough Lene and maybe we'd all like to go out on the lake on a Sunday sometime.

Even the one coming if that suited ye.

My two ears fill with rushing sound right inside them. The picture I drew of the boat in the morning. I made it like there was a storm in the water with lines of light blue and dark blue, even purple and black and all of that. If I'd known what I was doing I would have made it calm, but now it is coming true like the stories and it could kill us all together.

That would be lovely, wouldn't it children, says Mum.

There is a big pile of bones on the side of my plate, and I look at it and nothing else.

The fat left on them has gone white and I never even noticed it happen.

Good to see children eat like that, good to see an appetite. Make them big and strong.

Lord but they're so strange the three of them.

And next Sunday on the lake. Where did that come out of? Only to have something to offer them other than a bag of lamb chops. The lunch was over and I had nothing to say, only the lake came into my head. I need to get on to Willy Treacy now about his boat. Anytime you like, says he, but who knows what state he keeps it in? I'd look fairly stupid then. He's very particular though: everything has to be just so. The boat will be a decent job. But next Sunday might not suit him at all.

You wouldn't know what these people were thinking.

That gossin isn't one bit happy with me, poor child is worse than shy. The little tíogar *himself. He was quick enough with Ráth Chairn to be fair to him. The girl is so well brought up, so mannerly. Isn't he lucky to have two women minding him?*

Just staring at the wall now one hand flat on top of his head, his hair pushed up in a bunch. He looks like he might cry or scream or maybe he's only carrying on.

The sister and the mother aren't one bit bothered by it, so I'll just work around him.

– Are you finished with this?

I'll take it anyway, give him the old thumbs up. Not that he's paying any heed to me. All the bones scraped in together.

– Rosemary and Jasmin will be extraordinarily pleased.

I thought she was talking about two people the way she said it, took me a minute to cotton on it was the dogs. Some names for dogs.

The girl, B they call her, adds her bones to the pile.

– The animals will enjoy a feast second only to our own.

The voice you might hear off a judge or an auctioneer or someone like that only it's a little girl, and no hint of a smile either to give any indication she's codding someway.

Ah the little man is back in action, grabbing for the plate of bones.

– I want to give them!

– Outside! Both of you!

The girl hoists the plate up above her head. Like she's keeping a bundle dry wading across a river. The little man and the two little dogs go swirling after her.

It's only the two of us in the kitchen now.

Me and her.

The air gets very thick.

I THOUGHT TO GO TO DEATH it would be fighting and all of that and things would not be normal and the day would not be like it is all the days. But today is just the same and nothing special and no way to stop it. And now we are here down the lane and there is all the water.

If I stay in the van then nothing can go wrong. I tried everything but when Mum has decided enough is enough and you are not making any sense there is nothing to be done. I could not tell her about the picture, I could not open my mouth to say it and I don't know why. Maybe that is the way pictures and stories work, once you have made it you cannot change it because it is somewhere else.

Jerry Drain's head and shoulders is right out the window, and his hand is on the wheel rolling it a little left and a little right with his palm. He's backing the trailer with the boat on it down a long concrete bit into the water. In the mirror I can see the trailer start to go under, the water sinking it, lapping at the edges and the waves tiny splashing against the green scum cement.

He pulls the handbrake up hard, and turns at me.

I'm going to leave her running, you won't touch anything sure you won't?

He looks down at the handbrake, and yanks it higher up again with that noise. The engine is loud without him in the cab and everything vibrates—I hold my elbows with my hands and all around me is things to touch that I shouldn't.

In the mirror I watch them busy with the boat and Mum helping in a hurry. B is above them with her chin held with her thumb under it and the other arm folded. She is barefoot and her skirt is all flowers. She steps forward onto the stone bit and curls her big toes over the edge.

Jerry climbs back in and says good lad. We drive up and park, going round in a big sweep and the trailer making a bouncing noise, water swinging from the metal and dripping a line along the dusty ground like a wet marker.

Are you right there Michael?

I don't know why he's calling me not by my name. He comes round to my side and opens the door and is kind of singing now. Are you right there Michael, are you right? Do you think we'll be home before the night?

If I get out none of us will ever get home. I go still to stop everything happening and stare right ahead. Out of the corner of my eye I see him holding up his hands to lift me down, but I go even stiller. Mum and B are standing on the shore. Mum is tied to the boat with a rope and B is holding her hand. Jerry walks away and I hear him say that singing—tis all depending whether, the old engine holds together, and it might now Michael, so it might.

Mum comes to me looking cross and Jerry is putting a life jacket on B down by the boat. I don't move my eyes. Mum is all talking soft to begin with. She thinks I'm scared to go on the boat, but she doesn't know what I know. I can't open my mouth and I can't look. Her voice goes hard.

You can stay sitting in the van, that's fine by me. Lots of children would give their right arm to get to go out on a boat on the lake. You're being an ungrateful little boy.

She slams the door a bit and walks off.

I'm looking at them all through the windscreen, I'm looking through glass and the picture is behind glass. I wanted to rip it up, but Mum put it in a frame and hanged it on the wall in her bedroom. I don't know why I made it a storm, I could have made it a nice normal day.

I want to be with Mum and B even if—I don't want to watch it happening.

The life jacket smells like togs in a drawer. Mum does the straps and it's up under my ears like I can't move my head properly. I tell Jerry he should wear a life jacket and he says I am right but he doesn't put one on.

I go and sit up the front in the pointy bit and Mum and B are in the middle and Jerry is at the back, pushing us off and jumping in at the same time. He hands the engine down into the water and a little wind skims all the way across the lake in a chill.

Mum asks does he swim and he says he was never taught, that no one on the island ever went swimming. Mum says that's interesting because what with all the fishermen and all of that, and Jerry says if you fall into the Atlantic the quicker you go down the better.

If there's a storm it's not my fault he's not wearing a life jacket, but Mum's not either and I tell her to put one on too. I say what if there's a storm. Don't worry my darling she tells me and laughs, the water is flat as a pancake. I think of Lough Derravaragh when the water was flat like a pancake and the three men were tipped out of the boat and lost their heads.

Nil aon scamall sa spéir, Jerry announces, there isn't a cloud in the sky.

The sky is flashing not to look. Up there are birds, too high to know what they are, lots of them. When I close my eyes against the white sun, they are thin M shapes hanged in my head over and over just like I drew.

The engine kicks in as his elbow comes up the two times. I lift into the air and the boat will overturn, but it swerves too in an out curve, two lines of white streaming behind. It flatters out and we skid across the water, the wedge where I am bouncing a bit and the wind blowing my face. We race along and my eyes water, the shore moves away and we are out into the everywhere shining grey open.

It's too noisy for talking, but everyone is smiling, even B is, her eyes closed forward against the breeze and like she is smelling the air. Over the side of the boat the water is black that you can't see down into. I lie forward to let my hand in and it's thick and strong against my wrist. Under the water my hand is something else.

There is trees out far away surrounded by lake—an island but there's no land only trees. It looks like they are coming in a bunch out like flowers in a vase. I point at it and shout into the wind, the wind that takes my voice and pulls it away from my mouth.

Mum makes sit-down signs with her hands, but the boat slowly moves in the direction I'm pointing. I move my finger another way to check it's me and the boat comes back again to follow. Jerry is smiling at me his eyes two creases, and I nearly smile too but instead I stop pointing and sit down.

The boat slows and I can see green mossy land, roots tangling the edges and branches dipping. There's a forever silence as the engine cuts out and Jerry Drain tips it up out of the water. We are swift still and duck is shouted because the trees are coming. There's a scratching about my ears, my head down in the safe ship.

I'm up and I can touch the branches, they have a slimy green stuff on them that collects. I make sure to get it under every nail.

Mum says this is what Ireland was like before people came, every inch of the whole country covered in forest.

Where did all the trees go?

People cut them down and burnt them. They cleared land for farming, it all happened bit by bit over thousands of years.

We look into the forest, and see Ireland as it was afor people had sheep in fields and there was any gardens and houses and all of that.

How did the people come?

In boats just like this. What do you think was the name of the first person who stepped out of the boat and climbed into the forest?

Mum is telling that there was nuns on this island.

Did they not cut down the trees?

Jerry says they would have cleared the land too—these trees have all grown back since then. The trees are quick enough when the people go.

B looks at me like she knew that too, but she didn't.

So how do we know about the nuns?

Well people write things down, says Mum.

But how do we know they're not just stories and not true?

Paper never refused ink, says Jerry, good lad.

Mum and me both look at him to shut up.

They say there was even a school here once.

This would be a great place to go to school, wouldn't it chilren? Jerry is making a joke and B smiles to be polite. I don't because it is not funny and I will not lie.

Jerry puts his hands under my armpits to lift me and I turn my head to the side and shut my mouth tight like when there's a very bad smell. He says grab that branch and puts me in a tree so I can climb down into the forest.

It's not possible even to find the ground with my feet there's so many trees. Moving anywhere is hard, there's a little gap and then you have to go over a branch or under or over and under at the same time. They're mossy trunks and you can't get anywhere. B's hand is on my shoulder and she uses me to climb. She snaps through rotten sticks, and I catch her leg but she breaks free.

The grown-ups stay in the boat floating and me and B stop in a big fork of branches. It looks far already back out to where the blue is, you could stay hidden here for a long time. We can hear the voices—one low one, and Mum—but what they are saying is only muttering. I follow B on, it's easier to move higher up the trees, down near the ground you get jammed every second, so we climb and jump from branch to branch alone and no one could catch us if they tried.

Mum starts to call us, her voice is small. B goes towards it, but creeping. No breaking branches or making any noise. We come close enough to see Mum looking, but she hasn't seen us because her head is moving one way and then another.

Look at them there says Jerry, and he ruins everything.

Come on you two or you'll be left here. Mum is always in a hurry sometimes and impatient. Did you not hear me calling?

B says we could live here quite happily thank you very much. Mum says you wouldn't have anything to eat and Jerry says sure wouldn't they catch eels, Lough Lene is full of eels. B says about eels how they are like snakes but fish and they live underwater.

I keep my hand out of the water all the way back.

We climb into the van and B is in the middle and I'm on Mum's lap. Mum says, that was really really lovely thank you so much, and how lucky we were with the weather.

What is lucky is how I did not draw black in the sky, and only one little grey cloud.

The children had a great time, didn't you—and what do you say? Mum whispers this end bit so Jerry can't hear.

His door is open but he's outside. He's taking his boots and socks off and rolling his trousers that are wet up tight to below his knees. His feet and his ankles and his calves are very white like the roots of things sometimes under a rock when you lift it and you aren't supposed to see them. He wrings out his socks and his arms are brown and red, but his shins are that white. I can see his toenails that are bent.

Thank you says B, loud, and Jerry says you're more than welcome. I joined in with the *you*, so it sounded like I said it but I didn't really.

July

I go to the barn and take a whole bale of straw, there's loads and loads all new. Mum will say all you have to do is ask and all of that if she sees me, but I'm not asking him anything. The twine is sore on my hands so I get a rope from the garage and loop it through—this way I can pull the bale over my shoulder. It's a long way, all past the back of the sheds and round the house. And all the time Jerry Drain might come but I'm not scared of him.

When I wrote for him to go away he went, and I can do that any time. Even if he's always got a bottle of 7up when he comes to say hello.

With the sheet of corrugated iron on and all the straw, I can fit in the hole lying down but I can't turn over. I can just move my head from side to side. Light comes in through holes like bullet holes and just the smell of dirt and wet rust. This is my place and I can rest in peace here with no one disturbing me. I close my eyes to see the whole field everywhere above me, I'm right in the middle but it's all empty of me even I'm here just underneath.

I climb out and it's all blinking and Jerry Drain is coming across the field. His head is up looking at me and then his head is down looking at the ground, and he's coming straight at me. I never even heard the Dyna. You can see the straw poking out from under the galvanise and there's lots of bits round the field. He can't be sure it's his straw anyway, he has no proof. If I'd heard the engine I could have stayed in under the field.

He lifts up his head when he's close, and hello he says with the O bit like he's singing a song. He doesn't even look at the straw, just round at the tools lying on the ground and scratches behind his ear.

I hear you're building a fort out here. His voice is like he's talking to a little child. You have the foundations dug.

I'm not doing a fort, I'm doing an ambush, but the less he knows the better. He is planning something bad even pretending to be nice, and I will catch him out in the end.

He's lifting up the galvanise and having a look in, but maybe's going to go mad and kill me because why hasn't he said anything about his straw.

Is it foundations or what is it?

I don't know.

You don't know? He says *know* like *know-oh* like it's a rhyme. He says that it will fill up with water in a few days and it'll be a nice job then.

He doesn't know what he's talking about and it's a stupid thing to say, so I say no it won't and he just puts his bottom lip out but his mouth stays shut.

I brought a few things with me to maybe give you a hand. Come and help carry them.

I don't move and I watch him walk away.

Under his arm he brings in sheets of corrugated iron. He has fence posts and a big crowbar, a sledgehammer, a milk container cut open but still with the handle bit to carry it—full of those curvy nails with two points like two ends and no end. I have a look at them when he goes for more things. The nails are mostly old but there's a good few shiny new ones, you can see the cut metal to make the points on them, like when you sharpen a pencil with a knife not a sharpener and it looks better. He has a hammer with a ball shape on the back of it instead of a claw. The handle has green and yellow electrical tape wrapped around for grip. Up the Royals.

He drives the bar into the ground and doesn't hit any rocks. He twists it and turns it back and forward and then throws it down and picks up a fencing post. He stabs the point down in the hole, the post is new nearly—a good one.

Hold this steady for me.

I go and put my hand on it and he taps with the head of the sledgehammer a few times holding it with a short handle and the post goes in the ground a bit.

Don't move it now sure you won't, hold it steady.

With the sound of a switch his hands slide along the handle and he swings the sledge up high and down and the post makes a crack as it sinks in. I feel the clunk of it in my hand.

He takes a tape measure out that I didn't see he had.

Hold this end for me.

I don't move and he doesn't wait he just uses the clip thing and pulls out the yellow measure all the way along with a sheet-of-steel sound.

He kneels down and says three thousand and forty-five we'll call it three thousand and fifty but he is not talking to me. He measures from the post and waits with his thumb on the ground.

Bring me that bar there and we'll see how we are.

The long bar is heavy and I need two hands. He takes it with one hand and puts the end standing just beside his thumb.

We'll get this one fixed now and we mightn't be so bad.

He makes work the metal bar again and I hold the post again, and then he takes the sheet of corrugated iron and holds it up flat against the two posts.

Now hold this up so she doesn't fall.

As soon as I put my hand there, he lets it go. He takes the milk carton with the nails and drives them right through the sheeting at the low bits not the high bits. He does both sides, one at the top, one at the bottom and one in the middle. The metal is loud bangs and the Jacobs shock.

I wouldn't worry about those two.

We do another post, and the next sheet, and when he goes for the fourth one I can see he's doing a square, with my hide in the middle of it. He wants to know do I want a door, he can put a hinge on it. I stay quiet because I've no interest in his walls, let alone his door. He knows nothing and his fort will be the most sticking-out thing in the whole field—attackers wouldn't even have to climb to step over the walls. Some of the corrugated iron is rusty too, all red with it and you'd probably put your foot through it if you wanted.

I'm standing in the middle and he's got the last sheet up on its side.

Are you coming out or will I shut you in there?

I won't go his way, I can climb out here far away from him.

As I swing myself over I've too much weight, because it's higher than I thought and my leg is a bit hanging one side and then the other, so I have to push with my hand and I get it wrong. I feel the metal edge sink into my thumb and slice. There's no pain but a tingle in my whole bones and the cut is two sides open. It is normal thumb either side with a bit of soil in the lines of the skin, but where the cut is has white inside and yellow white and there's new pink. There's no blood. How can there be no blood? The pain comes ugly and I won't cry but the tears rise out of my eyes. I start running to the kitchen and it's all Jerry Drain's fault.

Mum says not to worry when I show her and I have to hold it under the tap. I'm too scared and she starts to get angry telling me to hold it under the tap right now. Jerry Drain's there coming in too and she says I have a bit of a cut on my thumb, it's nothing to worry about, but I know she knows how bad it is and that it's his fault. He stands there and she will tell him to go away but she doesn't.

Jerry Drain nods and goes out again and when he does I put my thumb under the tap. Mum is happy when I do it. It hurts but she says it doesn't hurt it's just the cold of the water. There is bits of green stalks and a big see-through plastic in the sink and the water makes noise on it.

There are flowers on the table that aren't like real flowers, they are like fake flowers with petals all the same size and all one colour like yellow and pink and no other colours in them like normal. They are so bright maybe it is plastic.

Are they real?

Are what real, darling? She wraps a plaster on all the way around.

Those flowers.

Well I wouldn't put them in water if they weren't real now would I?

The blows of the sledge are away out in the field, they rock and echo and they stop.

Where did they come from?

I know where they came from, and Mum says Gearóid brought them for me like it is why wouldn't it be. But we know it is bad and rotten and what does he think he is doing. He has gone too far this time. When it was him on the phone he said he would kill Mum and drown her and kill me then after and I do not forget that. I will never forget even if everyone else has. I am wounded and he will attack when we least expect.

I know Jerry Drain is downstairs because I hear voices like it is to hear just mumbles. It is too light outside to sleep even with the curtains and I listen but I cannot hear. I have to stay awake, if there is a scream I will go full pace. I think where my knives are, and my hurl is propped in the corner behind the dogs' armchair.

There is talking outside now and I am at the window, I do not move the curtains but through the slice I can see the Dyna and Mum and Jerry Drain and the door is open and he has a hand on the handle but he is leaned back to talk to Mum and they are up close and he kisses her on the mouth and his head is down and kissing and I will not watch this I do not want to watch this.

I throw my covers on the floor and I take my drawing pad with the cardboard back and a pencil on the big wide middle of the bed. I do not even need the light on to see and write it all the way it was and all the way it will be. The boy was making a hide and the enemy came to help thinking that he would win his trust and then be able to sneak in and destroy everything but he could not resist attacking and cutting the boy and how it was his sword hand but the little boy fought him nevertheless. The enemy was Jerry Drain but then he ate butter in the mornings with his hands so because his hands were slippy he dropped his weapons, the sword too. In the end the boy kills him and wins a great victory and it is over.

When I am finished I go to look at the window and the Dyna is gone and Jerry Drain is gone and everything looks like it should be and the dark is nearly down. I did not hear his engine go but I have made him disappear into thin air and if he ever comes back he will regret it. I cut out the page with my knife so it doesn't rip and my thumb throbs but it is not hurt, it is a beating wound that will be revenged. I fold the story once and twice, and I put it under my pillow. I lie down and I can feel it coming up into my head from under and my thumb throbs when my heart beats.

THERE IS A BIG ENVELOPE AND the colour of it is cream but cream is not that colour. I would not have any if the cream was like that. On the front is *School Report* and it says all how B is at school. Inside is bits of papers together, a hole in the corner and a green string going through. There is a little metal bar not to fall out. It is all different subjects and we read them together, I sit on Mum's knee and B beside. The writing is different on every page and some are with a typewriter but some are impossible to read and what does that word say, what could it be? It is definitely *i n* at the start, ha it is *industrious* yes it must be. B has an impressive grasp and a sharp intellect and diligent means not lazy. We always knew this but it is nice to see it written down. It is all amazing and well done but B does not even smile, she just looks like it is all normal and why not. She points to the top corner and says look I was not top in maths. There is one number over another and we did not realise what is was and but look at them all, they all say 1 which means she has come top. Now Mum is B this really is quite wonderful and all of that. B is a show-off saying she was not top in maths to show that she was top in all the others and still third in maths which is not bad either, and I know what she is doing even if Mum does not. It is lying like that. And now she wears shoes all the time and she has forgotten her feet.

She must like going away and being at school a bit because everything is Excellent and Bravo. One report is just that one word bravo and an exclamation mark and it is funny because the others spend a long time saying how good she is but this one just is written Bravo! in the middle. But Bravo! is not funny it is stupid.

Mum says right well we need a project to occupy us now there is no school all summer and maybe I can do more with my bit of garden. I tell her I want to keep it wild the way I like and she says we both know it's because I'm lazy and I don't want to do any work. But that's not true, she said I could do exactly what I wanted and she has to keep to that even if it's not what she meant. I like how my bit looks beside all the rows and no grass. Mum is getting cross with me and how after she is just all nice to B and I might cry—she said I could do what I liked with my bit of garden and now I am not to be clever. But I am right and she is wrong. It is not fair that it is bad when I am clever when clever is a good thing actually.

B says I hear you have a new fort, will you show me?

We go out and I want to try and catch the Jacobs and B says we're not to disturb them and she is different and I hate her. I do not want to go near Jerry Drain's fort that used to be mine. She is not listening though and goes anyway to it.

I lift up the sheet of galvanise over my hide to show her and let it fall back open. The water is right up to the edge and straw floating. Maybe I will bury Jerry Drain here, the hole is big enough and he would rot in the water and be under and hidden.

B says the fort is an impressive construction and who helped because she knows it was not me and I tell her Jerry Drain but I didn't want him to he is my enemy and she says oh. She is like Mum now saying it was a nice thing he did for me. I tell her the phone calls have not stopped and how it is him.

When I have explained she says it is not sure it is him actually and I have to be fair. But I can see she is worried and I am sorry I said, because she has her face like nothing in it, but lines on her forehead.

I want to say not to worry and tell her about the stories, but they are a thing deep down and they go deeper and deeper away. She would say that stories do not come true, it is impossible. But she does not know the truth. I will not actually kill Jerry Drain maybe but the story will and it is the story anyway. I don't tell B about the kiss either as it is too angry. It is all the things she does not know and it is like she will not chase the Jacobs. She is not here when things happen and when she comes back she has been gone and she does not remember how to be.

We go to hunt for pallets because Mum pays a whole 20p but nothing if they are rotten. I ask to B how she would kill an enemy and she says she does not answer hypothetical questions on a point of principle, it is not real and it is stupid. But I ask her and ask her and ask her and even she will not answer. I keep just asking and going and going and saying please and please and why it is not fair and all of that and I even put on a crying voice until I am in real about to cry. And she says really, you are really about to cry because I will not tell you my preferred method of killing an enemy and I wipe my eyes and try not to laugh. She says fine, I would use poison.

I would put poison in their food because no one has tasters anymore and that way you wouldn't be caught and go to prison.

Are you satisfied now she says, but I am thinking about poison. She knows Jerry is my enemy and she has said how to kill an enemy. She did not like to hear about the phone calls and ha ha ha—bravo B bravo bravo, I didn't even think of that.

While we're eating I put my elbows on the table and chew with my mouth open and then when Mum says elbows I hold them over but don't touch them down so they aren't on the table. I catch Jerry Drain with his elbow on the table but I don't say anything, I just nudge B and point. I do it so Mum and Jerry Drain see and I just say everything with my eyes, I lift my eyebrows a tiny bit to say for goodness' sakes.

I wait for a good space where everyone is quiet and I practise it a few times in my mouth, like getting ready to jump in the river, then one-two-three.

Mum, why is Jerry always here?

Everyone looks at me, Jerry is smiling with his forehead wrinkled up. His skin looks rubbery, like it's been scraped—you can see the little holes all smooth, but his neck is hairy down the side of his collar. B is with that look of when I kicked Rosemary too hard on purpose. Like maybe she won't talk to me or play with me for a long time and like it was her I kicked not the dog. She looks at Mum worried, as if I've broken something and we're both going to get shouted at. Mum's mouth is the teeth all shut and her eye twitches because she's choosing the right words. The air is cut when she speaks.

You know full well how desperately rude it is to talk about someone in the third person. You've finished eating so what you can do now is—

He's all right, I am always here. You want to know why I'm here? I'm always here because I like the three of ye.

He grabs my fist and lifts my arm, and he pokes where the ribs are. Mum's face stops being hard, and the poke tickles and he does it again. I can't help laugh, I don't want to but Mum laughs and B is looking like she will talk to me again. He stops the tickling and I stop the laughing, but he doesn't let go of my fist.

I try to open Jerry's fingers but I can hardly move them at all. There's gingery hairs on the backs of them, and I get my thumb, I have my right hand free which is good because that's my strong one, and I get my thumb in under his little finger. I can lift it a bit but just to the first bend. I try them all at once but there's no way, he's not even having to tighter his hand, they just won't budge.

I laugh at the strength of it. I let my arm go and it hangs there between us like a rope, then I yank it suddenly—but it's stuck. Mum and B aren't watching, they're clearing plates and at the sink and all of that. I'll get my hand back though. In the soft side of the wrist, between the bone and the stringy bits. In there hurts. I must be getting the wrong place because he smiles and shakes his head. I search for that right bit and I use my long thumbnail I have. If you cut your wrist you can be dead in two minutes because that is directly straight to your heart. Maybe I will cut his wrist with my nail and all the blood will drain out of him. That is how he will be dead and I will kill him like this in an accident and now is the story happening. But his stringy bits are like steel under the skin. Even though I'm in the right place where it hurts, it's no good at all. He raises his eyebrows but it's because he's interested in my ways—there's nothing like pain, no ow or anything like that.

His knuckles are just white, and there's creases like in clothes of red. Some of the skin on the back of his hand is all little cuts and sore looking. There's the cracks going in both directions and straight, and I hit there, and I bring my knuckles down on his knuckles, but it just hurts me.

The table is clear but the serving spoon that wasn't used in the end is I can reach. It's heavy, I know it from the weight of it that I have won now. I give a ha ha ha laugh and wave it about. He doesn't let go so I use my eyes to motion, to bring his eyes to his hand and the big heavy spoon I have. I do it a few times and do another ha ha ha for warning. But he is just looking at me, like that's it, there's nothing to be done and things are the way they are, it is what it is. I lift up the spoon to show I'm going to hit with it and he understands, there's no way he doesn't understand. I've warned him.

I hit his knuckles, not hard because it's very sore doing that and I don't want to be in trouble. He still doesn't let go, so I hit him again, hard. It's no good so I hit him harder. It makes an awful bone sound, but he has to let go he can't hold on to me and I hit him again and again—I'm aiming and bringing the spoon down as hard as I can, over and over. My aim goes bad because I'm hitting him so much, but every most times there's that bone sound. Maybe I will crush and break his bones and the spoon will give him tetanus and his tongue will come out all stiff of his mouth and his jaw will lock and he will take weeks to die. It will be his fault because he wouldn't let go. But he doesn't even blink, just stays smiling, his eyes all over my face. I know the pain of how sore it is but he does not feel pain. He is not a human even. He is so strong he can kill us all and even all three we could not fight him.

I'm about to cry now when I wasn't just afor. I cannot ever have my hand again and my head is tight and my skin all shrinks. My hand is as much mine as me and I can't get it back. He sees my eyes because of tears coming too much to blink and he lets me go. I'm blinking for the tears but some go out and on my cheek. My fist feels like a poppy, when it's trying to open and the curled petals can be seen careful in the thin split of the bud. The skin is white and blotched red where the blood is under. I grab the fingers out and back and it is strange. His smile goes and he's confused looking, and sad like even maybe. His eyebrows meet, foxed together and he says sorry lad. I didn't mean to upset you, I just wanted to hold your hand.

That'll swell in the morning, be bad for a day or two. Hurts to close it. Nobody will notice me flexing it under the table. She's too busy looking daggers at me. I can't let any of the hurt into my face, she'll think I'm feeling sorry for myself.

– Are you alright? she's saying quietly. And him busy pretending nothing happened. The very last thing he wants is for me to see him crying. He runs in next door and she goes after him.

At least when he was hitting me, I could smile, stretch it out into something else. Is the knuckle broken? I can close it and open it so it should be OK – if I can work it today, I can work it tomorrow.

B is finishing the wash up, she knows when to stay out of things. I'll go and dry the dishes.

This isn't easy on him, poor lad. My own father was gone when I was his age, gone a few months. It's not the same though – his is still out there somewhere. But then I thought mine was as well. No man came into the house after.

The fist aches when I close it on the towel. This will slow me down tomorrow. And I have a blot on my copybook. And that poor young lad was crying because I wanted to hold onto him. He might have cut the hand from me and I wouldn't have let him go.

B hands me a sudsy plate.

– Get on with it, she says.

Because Jerry is over again there's no reading all together by the fire. He has the good chair where B and I used to sit. Mum says I can go on her lap, and sometimes I do and when she's talking I tickle her. But she won't put up with my nonsense and she says she wants to hear Gearóid. I go and sit on the carpet at the corner of the fire. My thigh is too hot very quickly but I'm blocking the heat from him, and I just have to move now and again to not burn my leg too much.

The fire spits.

Chestnut is bad for that. Jerry leans to get the ember and throws it back in afor I can lick my fingers to pick it up. He does it with bare fingers and no spit but it does not burn him.

He's talking about the island he's from called Inishmaan, he's always talking about his island. He's being stupid on purpose telling B that Ireland is an island off the Aran Islands. B makes her face that she will not be tricked but smiling, and she never smiles. He talks to Mum about how they made fields out of rock, how the whole island is limestone and they used to break it up with iron bars and stuff the cracks with whatever they had. They'd load the donkey with seaweed and sand and bring it up and mix it into the broken rocks. And that would turn into a little bit of soil then over years.

There was no such thing as electricity and when there was clear nights they used the moonlight for working with. When the electric came the cable was brought only as far as the house and then they had to figure out how to use it, sitting round a table with all the bits laid out in front of them.

And how everything was precious, even the cowpats. They used to pick them up when they could and stick them in the holes in the wall to dry. That way they'd have firing, there was nothing ever wasted.

Why did you leave? says B and I do a laugh, because I want to show why did he leave if he is always on about it so much. But no one even looks at me and everyone is all listening to him. He says he left so he could go working, and he had to learn English when he came to the mainland. He's worked on farms in Limerick, Tipperary, Roscommon, Offaly, Cavan, Wexford, you name it he's worked there. Laois, down in Carlow, over in Leitrim.

I have a wooden map like a puzzle with all the counties different colours, Waterford is an upside-down duck and the piece is missing. When he names a county I see the shape and the colour, and I see where it goes in the map.

Jerry says he's no different truth be told to the tinkers parked down the road but then no one is really, there's not many people stay put. He looks around the room like it's the first time he's been in here and says there's people gone from this house to every corner of the world, scattered all ov—

The world is round, there's no corners when it's round.

That makes him stop, ha. B looks at Mum but Mum isn't giving any looks, she takes a log from the basket and puts it on the fire.

What about there? He's pointing behind the log basket, where the fireplace joins the wall. It's only shadow, a bit of cobweb and a dark triangle in behind. There could be anything down in that black bit, like when the dogs try to get their noses in somewhere.

There's one corner there.

He points at the far side of the room.

There's another corner there. And they're all different from one another. Even two corners of the same room. You as well, you've travelled, it's not just these corners you've lived in. You weren't born in Meath, you were born up in Dublin. You were in Westmeath and you were in Limerick. You were in Kilkenny and in Mayo. He says Mayo like the end O is the important bit.

How does he know where we've been? Does he know we nearly went to England and the school lunch had custard so disgusting we had to come home to Ireland? Mum must have told him things. What else has she told him that isn't his? When we were in the commune and all the children needed to move the grain hopper so we stood round it in a big circle and all lifted at once and we carried it right the way across with no adults. He doesn't know how good that was. Or doing poohs in a bucket and having newspaper cut up in squares to wipe with—that horrible smell in the wooden place, does he know about that? Does he know about the park boys in Limerick and how it wasn't safe to go in the playground and how they came into the school with a gun? I don't know what he knows and what he doesn't know and I hate him.

I want to say why don't you go back to where you came from? The words are in my head and I move my lips to them when no one's watching.

August

We have a big job to help Mum and it is exciting to go in the car. I find out too late it is to help Jerry Drain and we are in his yard but he is not there. Mum is moving big metal bars and gates to make a wall and yanking at them, and me and B just watch.

I am to stand in the middle of the road and when the sheep come they will see me and go in the gateway and into the yard. They won't go past me. If I am worried I can wave my arms and shout, sheep are easily directed. Once the first ones go the others will all follow, they are not bloody-minded like the Jacobs. I am scared for if a car comes but Mum says don't be silly. I just have to hold up my hand and don't worry it will stop. It's very important because it will help and block the way, but if I let it by it might drive the sheep up the Athboy road and that would be a disaster. B says how do you know they won't go up there anyway when they come to the junction and Mum says they know the way.

I can see them coming, and they are going quick and all together trotting and rumbling, filling the road full up and even going past each other and squeezing in the hedges crackling and tripping a bit up on the grass and moving faster the closer they are, and it is their breathing I can hear. I can't block the whole road and it is they will not stop.

They slow at the junction where everything widens out and the lead one comes forward and then towards where I am and they will not go past me so I spread up my arms and wide and shout yah yah so it is to know to go in the gate when it gets to me, but the sheep's head dips down and it stops on its legs. It turns and twists and gives two jumpy kicks up in the air and goes running, and they all follow with it and pour away in the wrong direction up the Athboy road. Mum behind them is screaming and waving her arms, you stupid stupid boy. It is the disaster happening but if I run by them I can bring them back.

But they go faster away in front and stop stop what the hell are you doing?

It is the sheep that are stupid not me and I stop but the sheep have gone away around the bend.

Mum is red in the face and her teeth together, and B is looking at me that it is okay but I am not to cry or make a noise. I am just to wait for the shouting to stop and say sorry, and I keep my head down because otherwise it can make things worse.

But no shouting comes. Mum's face is not angry, she is her arms folded and eyes open wide. She shakes her head and we go to her close. She is quiet and I do not know what is happening, it is her face but it is sad like when the mink got the chicks but worse. B puts a hand touching on her arm but not holding with her fingers just straight and says what's wrong but not out loud.

Mum looks to the sky and to the ground and she can't bring the words maybe. She looks after where the sheep have gone and where they were supposed to go.

What kind of woman will he think I am if I can't even bring in a few sheep?

And it is Jerry Drain will be angry with her and he is making her sad and scared and it will not go like this I will not allow it. He is torturing her. Enough is enough.

There are honks and car horn honkings and back come the sheep and oh thank God oh thank God, quickly, quickly out of the way. There is a car slowly coming behind the whole herd of sheep and we stand and woosh them in the yard and they are jumping one on another to get in and oh thank God for that.

There is a horrible little teddy on the kitchen windowsill. I didn't see him but I know Jerry brought it. It is all white and on the paws is red with love hearts and when I said where did that come from Mum said where do you think and I did not answer because we both know very well. My knife is so sharp that you cannot see where I stuck it in unless you pick up the teddy and look. If Mum sees the cut I will just lie like all the lies she tells. The teddy looks alive but he is dead like Jerry will be dead. Jerry is always being all lovely with Mum and she is smiling even when he is not here but I know it is all trickery and lies. He is tricking her but he will not trick me.

Mum is making a remedy. When I woke up in the morning I heard the tap tap tap, and she is still going now. Her eyes are closed and she is counting and the kitchen is all powerful. The table is empty and she is tapping the tube on the leather book. Her arm is flexing and the tube is pocking. B goes away to read and I go in and out but Mum does not even maybe see me when she is counting out the healing.

But next time she is rubbing her arm and on a break and I ask her who the remedy is for.

It is for Gearóid.

Her voice is that she is busy like I am not to talk. She does the tubes and says do you want to help but I shake my head. I do not know what she started with to make the remedy and what is wrong with Jerry Drain. This must be the story working. It usually comes true straight away and it's a long time already it existis. Maybe he will be dead and I will not have to touch him. If he is a patient then there's something weak and I will discover it. He doesn't smoke like Mrs Lynch so he is not addicted, but I will find out.

I don't see anything wrong with him. It is what I am saying but a question too with how I have my voice.

It's not always something you can see. Mum rubs her shoulder underneath her jumper.

He just thinks he has to work harder and it will go away. Mum is nodding her head, slowly like how she taps the tube. I look at the little dent in the book where the tap has been over and over.

Can you imagine thinking you don't work hard enough when all you do is work?

I do not know what is going on and why Mum is sad, and Jerry Drain is always making her unhappy. And it is all lying but I have caught them out now.

So why did he come to you if he just has to work?

Mum smiles but not like I have won, it is as if there is so much I do not know.

No, Gearóid would never complain. He's not the complaining type. Sometimes, when you're close to people, you can see things they can't see themselves.

She closes her eyes and it is too late for me to talk. The tube brings down on the book and she counts the measure after every tap.

Will you do me a favour?

I do my head to the side to say I am listening.

Will you go up the fields to Gearóid for me and give him this?

The remedy is ready in the little plastic pot and on the table.

Tell him the same instructions as for Mrs Lynch.

Why do I have to go?

You don't have to, I thought you might like to. Her voice is all not getting angry but it is really.

Why would I like to?

You may not, I don't know. I just thought maybe it would be nice for you.

Why would it be nice for me?

I don't know, you might like to spend some time with Gearóid.

I smile like it is a joke.

Why are you making a sarcastic face at me? Why wouldn't you like to spend some time with him? Oh forget it, you may forget it, I'm sorry I asked.

But I take the pot in my hand and I go out. I don't go round to the fields though. It is like I will but then I go around the far side of the sheds the other way. I have it in my fist. I don't know why I am going the wrong way but it is happening. I don't know where I am going and I go to the garage to my secret place where I keep my axe.

I am standing in front of the rat poison.

My skin is when someone walks over your grave and the no noise is loud in my ears. I am not me anymore I am the boy in the story and it is him that is here and I can just watch. It is like with the axe and the hosepipe and the axe is here too and I know why I cut the hosepipe now. It has all already existis. Like dreams where you don't remember until things are that they've been afor. I know like it is already afterwards.

I can feel me as I go back to the kitchen and I do not hide because I know Mum is gone, and I am opening the cupboard under the sink because there is the yellow gloves Mum never uses but are for washing up. That they maybe belong to the Pinks. Even the gloves no one ever uses are making sense why they are there all along. I am taking a long spoon too, when you sup with the devil you use a long spoon and what is happening is bad but it is only the story not me and it is like it is already and it is just anyway. I am not breathing and it is like being very scared but I am not, I am watching from the corner of the ceiling.

I pour half the sugar with the cure in it in the sink and wash it down so it melts away. And then I am here again I am in the garage and the yellow gloves are too big and cold inside and like wet but there is no water. I see my hands and they are cold and rubber and bright yellow and not mine at all and the box is in both hands to put it on the ground. In the light the poison is not dark blue like I thought. It is light blue but not a blue that's the same to anything, it is its own evil blue. Blue like fire but dull like ash after. It crushes up small on the concrete. The back of the spoon is covered with the dust of it and even I will have to throw the spoon away after maybe. From the powder heap I can see the spoonfuls careful, going in the little pot. Some poison is on the yellow fingers of the glove and I can feel the heat through the rubber but nothing really touches me.

It is all the same and I clean the floor with splashing water. There is a fizz even and bubbling and more water quickly. The floor is stained but it is the floor and all dust and dirt anyway. I take the gloves off inside out and hide them by the axe. I do not know where to hide the spoon so I put it in the box and it is like when there is a spoon in the cocoa and you think you have lost it so you get another but then the spoon is in the box all along.

I walk across the fields not thinking of anything because I am not there, I am just shaking the pot in my fist and counting all the numbers in order one after the other.

Jerry Drain is making new a fence. He sees me and works again and looks up when I am close. I stand and he winks and I think for a second that he knows what is happening. But he does not know, he is only in the story, it is me that wrote it. Only to wink because he knows I cannot wink. Like if he whistles I cannot do it and spit comes out if I try.

Are ye well?

I think of how B would be, she knows how to talk when it is polite.

I am fine and how are you?

Mighty. Never better.

I hold out the pot.

Is this for me?

He does like wipes his hands on his hands, over the knuckles and pulling his thumbs through his fists.

It's very good of your mother to think of me.

He takes the pot and puts it in his front pocket straight away. I tell him the instructions the same to they always are, no food or water twenty minutes afor and after and not to ever touch it, just tip a little into the cap. Except I do not say let it dissolve on your tongue I say swallow it straight away. Because maybe it will burn. I don't know. And he is listening to me and he will do as I say and I want to smile too much to stop—I thought it was impossible and there was nothing that could be done with him being always everywhere and never going away but now I will be rid of him once and for all. It is easy.

How often am I to take it he asks, and I say five times a day. Even if Mum said only morning and evening—she said that but I say what I want to say and I can change whatever I want and Jerry Drain even says thanks lad and I am away running afor I laugh.

I do not look back once, my legs are skipping under me and I go faster, my heart is beating again catching up for when it stopped. I am much too fast to ever be caught.

What makes it blue I wonder? Is there some other plant in it? Only sugar and water she said, and the essence of what troubles you.

I only spat in a tub of water, that was all she wanted from me, and now I'm crippled in a ball with the cramp.

Is this what I need? Will this root out the lack in me? My nose bleeding, the taste of iron in my mouth. Blood now on the straw when I spit. Will fighting this give me the strength I need? Look – now – I can stand. What kind of power is this? I can stand now I put my mind to it. I can wipe my nose and I can walk and what is stopping me only ever myself. I can stretch through this pain and I can keep going. Look at this – one foot, and now the other.

She warned me. Said things often have to get worse before they get better, but I don't know did I ever feel as sick in my life.

Me and B are eating peas. There isn't enough really for freezing. We can just go when we like and eat them in the garden but be careful not to damage the plants. B picks them because she says I pull them and they break and we'll get in trouble.

When she's picked one she gives it to me. I split the pod and pull them all off at once with my thumb and I give her handfuls from my fist into her palm. Sometimes the tiny little ones at the top don't come and I get them with my mouth. The ones that are tight and too full squeezing the pod are no good and not sweet. We eat them anyway, but you know they are not going to be good. They are hard to open even and don't split along the right bit, they have to be broken in two and they are a waste more than anything.

Mum says come here you two, I have to tell you something.

Her face is serious. I had forgotten all about Jerry Drain and all of that, but now I remember in a rush and everything and it is tingling everywhere. Now she will tell us Jerry Drain is dead and we won't be seeing him again.

She is kneeling down weeding carrots. My last pea is a big dry one that is even a bit white and I chew the bitter taste going over.

You know the Pinks are coming soon for their summer holidays.

B nods and it is not what I was about to hear, it is not Jerry Drain dead, it is the Pinks. We have to leave when the Pinks come. They prefer if we're not there when they arrive. We always go to Granny and Grandfather England's and it's a long way.

Well this year we aren't going to go to England.

It's very hot in Devon and the roads are narrow and steep, the hedges are really high and they grow on top of banks of earth. The road is low down like a stream in shade but sometimes the tarmac melts at the top of the hill by the five-acre field. It sticks to my shoe and leaves a footprint on the road. I push it off with pebbles. There are ferns and foxgloves under the hedges and the soil is dark red, it has been scraped along and red soil is not something you'd believe until you saw it, but it's true dirt. The ferns are so thick you can lie in them like a bed. The streams are clear and the rocks shine same to in water even when they're not. They are like wet rust and iron but they are stones.

I do a yesssss.

No, says B, we are not going. She said we are not going.

Mum is shaking her head, I'm sorry darling, I know you love it but it can't be helped.

Will we stay maybe with Aunt Sarah instead?

Aunt Sarah walks hound puppies so she has puppies forever. They always have names that start with the same letter like Ruby and Randall. The smell in the kennels is the worst smell in the world. There's pigs in England too and they love the power hose on their backs, the happy grunting noise they make is so happy it's inside you too. Aunt Sarah drives in the car and we go one hundred miles an hour, she tells us to look at the speedometer and she goes up past one hundred on the straight by the wall at the bottom of the hill to the bend. There's no one on those roads and anyway if you're going fast enough it's the other car that comes off worse. The puppies are for the hunt and Grandfather England is master of hounds. On the walls are the heads of foxes and the doors are held open with horses' hooves. The bit where it was chopped from the horse's leg is covered in silver like icing on a cake. On the wall too in the corridor are brass hunting horns and me and B stood on a chair to take them down, we tried to blow but they wouldn't make the right sounds, just spitty air. Grandfather caught us and B went all white and we were very scared for a second, but he took a horn and puffed his cheeks and blew and the sound bulged out huge loud. It turns my stomach over that even when I think about the sound when it's not there it comes up from my tummy into my chest and fills it.

No, says B, listen. That is Devon too, we are not going to England—that is what you are being told.

I'm sorry my darlings.

B knows always the right questions.

Why are we not going?

We can't afford it, and to be very frank with you I don't want to. Mum has gone talking like she is about to be angry if we don't do what we're told right now but we haven't done anything.

How do you not want to? It is not fair, it is the best.

B is pulling at my jumper but I wriggle out.

Have you ever thought maybe I don't like it?

Mum's hand is full of weeds and she thumps it on the ground so the dirt comes off not to waste it.

One day you might realise that not everything is about you.

I do not say anything because she is sniffing in that way a little bit and her mouth is closed tight so if it opens that will be it.

The knees of her jeans are all mud and shiny and she kneels back down to the weeding with both hands in among the carrot tops seeing what is bad.

B looks at me to say don't talk I will talk. She uses her goody-goody voice.

Where will we go when the Pinks come, Mum?

Well that's the good news, we don't have to go far. We're just going up the road to stay in Gearóid's caravan, won't that be fun? Her face is smiling and her voice is won't that be fun and all of that.

We are going to stay in Jerry Drain's caravan. And it is happening really, I was right and Jerry Drain is dead. His caravan is empty and we will have it now he is gone, and maybe we will have his yard too and all his sheep.

B does not know anything yet, she is not always the one knowing.

And where is Gearóid staying?

Gearóid will go in where the sheep go in the winter.

It is not true again. He is alive again and I have not killed him. Maybe he will know and take revenge and it is a trap now. B is frowning.

That doesn't sound very suitable.

Don't worry, he doesn't really mind where he sleeps, he's not that kind of man. And it's just for a few weeks, he has a place to lie down in there for when they're lambing anyway. He showed me and it's comfortable enough.

THIS IS THE WORST HOLIDAY EVER. It is not a holiday we are not even anywhere. We are not allowed to go in our fields, nearly just the other side of the road, or down to the river to the swim place. It is the one thing we have to promise not to do, to go into our own fields. And we are certainly not to even think about going near the house under any circumstance. It's not our house when the Pinks are there and they don't want to be disturbed. But the fields and the house is two things not one thing.

I do not like to be in the caravan. It smells not like anything else and it is always be careful please be careful, this is not ours that is not ours. We eat at the table that is very cleverly also a bed upside down in the evening, and we are all in sleeping bags and me and B one end and Mum the other. There is even a little fridge and cupboards up high that snap shut for clothes.

B just reads and spends all day reading and she gives me ones she says are good but they are impossible. They have no pictures, even on the covers. Red books with gold writing on them. The last one was Northanger Abbey and it's too boring for one page even. Jerry Drain has lots of Westerns with good covers of cowboys and dust and I read them even if B tuts and does eyebrows up and down.

There is nothing to do in Jerry Drain's yard, not even any jobs. There's a washing machine though. It is in where the sheep shed is and when Jerry Drain is away and he's always away doing welding and all of that I go and look in the shed. There is a cot where he sleeps and there is a kettle and a dirty mug with a teabag in it. There is one little white plate with blue all around the edge. He lets us use his washing machine and he must be rich and have money hidden everywhere if he has a washing machine as they are very expensive.

At home we wash the clothes in the bath. We rub soap on the dirty bits and make fistfuls either side, then rub the two bunches together. It takes a long time to do it properly and my sleeves always get wet even when I roll them up over the elbows and then it's wet and tight on my arms. Wringing out is fun though. Mum takes one end and I take another and we twist in opposite ways. The water comes out bigger for big twists and it gets tighter and tighter and twistier and twistier. When there's no more drops to come out it's kind of dry but not and there's marks in it from the twisting. It's very flat and ready to go on the line where it won't take long. It is all very helpful and good to do a job well and be a help. When I have killed Jerry Drain dead I will find where he has hidden his money. I will buy Mum a washing machine, and I will buy a TV and I will buy all books for B.

I sit in front of the machine when it's on. It is up on a pallet and there's a very clean smell there right up close not like everywhere else. In the glass, if you don't look through it but into it, when the machine is on and the dark swirl colours and bubbles are moving, inside the glass there is a galaxy of space.

Above near the machine there is a little square of mirror stuck to a wooden post and there is a basin like for washing up. If I climb up I can look in the mirror and practise winking but it is always both eyes at once even if I hold one open and it is blinking not winking. Can you wink with this eye says Jerry Drain. And no you cannot, it's my eye. He wouldn't be winking at me if he knew the story that was happening. He can wink with his eye all he wants he will be dead and gone soon and the Pinks will be gone and we can go back home and everything can be normal again.

I am allowed to go see Mrs Lynch at least so I go there, I pedal fast past our gateway. I don't have a real reason to knock on Mrs Lynch's door and so I say are you cured.

I'm off them this good while now.

You have to walk very slowly behind Mrs Lynch otherwise you bump into her.

Her photos are out on the table. She keeps them in the yellow paper wallet with KODAK written on it. While the kettle is on, she finishes going through them and then puts them back. She doesn't show me them and I don't look, I watch her face but her face doesn't move, sometimes just the lips like she is saying some words but not speaking. Like when I have to say thank you to Jerry Drain and all of that. When she's poured the tea she sits down. She puts a hand flat down on the yellow pack of photos, takes her nose up at the top at her eyes between her finger and thumb and closes her head down.

I have two sons gone from me, she says. At least one of them is in heaven with the innocents. The first boy, the eldest—whose pushbike you have—Pat's mother was there hovering all the time I was pregnant on him. I knew she was up to something but I didn't know what. And then those few days after he was born, when she came in to see him, I realised what it was she'd done. I think it was the only time I ever saw that woman smile. A gift from God is what she said. You've been blessed. But it was a gift from the Devil is what it was.

Mrs Lynch is tears running down her cheeks, but she's smiling and nodding.

Never mind where he came from—he was a gift. It's true that he was a gift. Oh, and then when she saw I was that happy with him all the same, and that Pat was happy with him, it stuck in her teeth something rotten.

Mrs Lynch takes a handkerchief from her apron and blows her nose. She folds it to put it back.

Then the second time I wouldn't have her near me. There was nothing Pat could do only I wouldn't have her in the house—I said she comes in one door I'll go out the other one. It was like that the whole nine months. And then didn't it kill her outright seeing the perfect son I had the second time. He wasn't three weeks old when she gave up the ghost. I was only able feed him those three weeks, it was at the funeral my milk stopped coming in. That was her way of saying goodbye—she cut the milk from me.

Mrs Lynch puts two hands on the table to stand up, and takes the photographs away. There are no ashtrays about, I look at the edge of the sink and by the stove and on the table and I don't see any. I can't smell the Majors, the smell is only of turf and a little bit of soup. She's rid of them for good. She has a biscuit the same to me while we have the tea and she talks then about her son's wife, that woman, and all the shame that is in it the way she goes on with herself. And her son treated like he's no better than … she won't even say the word, she leaves words like that for other people. Words like that won't come out of her mouth.

Anyway that one is rightly served now, it's Father Farrell himself sends someone with a car to bring me up to Mass now she won't.

I am nearly finished my tea but I do not want to go back to Jerry Drain's yard. I can't go home and when I have one more sip the tea will be gone and I will have to go out.

You're not gone to England this year? Mrs Lynch waits to the end sometimes until she says anything that is important and we can talk about how unfair it is.

I'm not even allowed go near the river, and I'm not allowed in our fields.

You're not in the house at all?

No, we're up in Jerry Drain's yard, in his caravan.

You're all in with Jerry Drain? Mrs Lynch is smiling and I don't know why she is smiling.

No, he sleeps in the sheep shed.

He's inside in the sheep shed, he is?

She's asking a question even though I just told her, and she's nodding like she knows so why is she asking.

I hate him. I say it too late to stop and Mrs Lynch laughs.

You'll fight him I suppose. You will?

It is fierce and true and I look at her now she knows and she is staring in my eyes and she wants an answer.

I'll kill him.

Mrs Lynch chuckles and nods and huh-ho huh-ho, you will I'm sure. He has gone and put a lot on his plate that man. Heaped it, he has.

❧

It is dark though I am awake like it should be morning. I cannot see the ceiling but I listen and B is breathing and she is not and she is breathing.

I sit up and call for Mum and there is no answer. In my sleeping bag I have my torch, so if I am ever scared in the night I can have my own light. When I switch it on the beam is at the door and the bit where is the little sink. I move it to where Mum is in her bed at the other end that is a sofa and a table in the day. Her sleeping bag is there and ripped open and empty and Mum is gone. I shine the light all round and she is nowhere and her pillow is there but she is gone. I have seen this all and the scream comes up from a memory that was not there till now. I scream Mum and Mum and when there is no scream I scream again.

Mum and Jerry Drain think I am not listening. They are sitting at the table by the window that is where Mum sleeps but is now all lunch and sandwiches again with white slice so it is amazing. I could eat white slice every day forever and I can sit with the door open and my legs out and on the breeze block and look at the hedge. Every bite is ham and butter and the white slice in my teeth. And they talk like I am not there. If their voices go a bit low I am listening more. B cannot hear anything sometimes when she is reading and her eyes are just on the page and her face is nothing only reading.

Mum's low voice says how is the remedy working and my skin in under my hair goes tight. It is how Red Indians do, that is the bit they take with their knives. It is scalping and being scalped. They gather and you can't hear them in a circle round you but they are there. I am like them, hidden, and I will have a scalp.

Jerry makes the sound of drinking tea and one plate on another.

It's the best thing ever. I could do with some more of it actually.

Already? That was quick. When Mum frowns I can know without looking by her voice. Once in the morning and once in the evening?

The young man told me as many times a day as possible.

I can feel them looking at my head. I eat another bite of sandwich and do not turn around. I can't chew though, everything is stuck. Why is he not dead already? If he wants more I will do the same again easy. Maybe Mum's remedy to make him well mixed in worked against the poison.

Well it's no harm. But isn't that funny. He must want you to get better quickly.

Jerry makes a laugh through his nose and I feel like I will laugh too, but I bite more sandwich to stop it.

Why does that make you laugh?

I don't think he's altogether too fond of me, really.

That's not fair. He's a very sweet boy deep down.

Jerry makes another laugh, but this one isn't really, it's scoffing and scorn.

Well why else would he want you to take the remedy? Her voice is a bit when news headlines are on waiting for

The Archers. When she is about to be angry the words are very clear and one by one sharp. It is extra polite but not at all. He is for it now.

But there is only a long quiet—I do not even chew though my mouth is full with both bites.

And then Mum's voice is for when we had better change the subject. He has had a lucky escape.

September

When we come home the Pinks are gone and our house is so beautiful that I forgot. The Virginia creeper is a darker green and the grass needs mowing because it is long. There's a dog pooh near the back door. The pooh is on the outside and on the inside. Something has squashed a bit of it flat—the inside pooh is yellow and soft and the outside pooh is crusty. Everything is the same. The same floorboard creaks in the corridor and the rooms are all the way they are. But there's apples like we've never had, a whole bowl of them on the windowsill in the dining room. They look like fake apples, the green skin shiny to plastic, and too big for what is normal. The skin shoves up under my lip and the crunch stings my teeth. I unload the spit onto the back of my hand and put the apple back.

I go along the river with B right the way until we see Trim. On the way back and near where the swimplace is there is a dead pig in the water. It's trapped in the tree branches but too far to touch even with a stick. We find stones to throw and I hit it first. The stone goes right into the side of the pig with a noise, it's not a thump or a squelch but it's both at the same time.

Walking in I hear Mum tell B that she has to be brave. They both stare at me and Mum looks like I've done something wrong. B's face is straight like she will cry. She doesn't ever unless we're fighting. The last time was when I hit her on the head with the stick and it wasn't an accident. She nods to Mum and tries to look like she is happy with a smile but all shut mouth.

She can do her own tie now. She told me she'll show me how when I have to go. Next year I'll be the same age she was when she went.

The tie is dark blue with red stripes on it and her shirt is too white to look at. She has a haircut for going back. It is short because Mum tried to get each side the same length and it is just below her ears now—it looks a little bit uneven because it is wet but it will be absolutely fine when it dries. It's called a bob. There is a very straight parting right down the middle of her head.

B is not really talking much, just nodding at the things Mum says, but when I stand on her toe she tries to hit me so I know she is okay. Mum says to say goodbye and wants us to hug but we won't. B's face changes back to normal and she says behave then walks off.

Mum is taking B to school and I am to stay with Jerry. It is stupid because I used to stay on my own so why is Jerry looking after me now? And when we stayed in his caravan he went to sleep in the shed—but now he is staying in our house we have not gone to sleep in the shed we are still in the house with him.

He is the only one allowed to answer the phone and the phone calls have stopped now. So it is no coincidence. I even said to Mum to show her why. She said when the coward heard a man's voice he went away. But it is all too clever and she thinks Jerry is protecting us, but he is the man on the phone too, he is the danger and it is no coincidence. It is so obvious but Mum doesn't see. Jerry cannot make phone calls to the house if he is in the house. I am the only one to know.

And I can hear him going to the bathroom at night beside my room, I know it's him because when he pees he pees straight into the water and it makes an awful sound. I pee on the white of the bowl and sometimes at the end it goes in the water and that's a bit rude by accident, but he must do it on purpose. And he says loadies instead of pooh and that is disgusting. He has no manners whatsoever.

He's taken B's room at the other end of the corridor. And Mum's gone in there with him. He swapped the beds around walking up and down through my room with them all in pieces. B's room is Mum's old room now—she gets the warm room because she's a girl, even though she is away at school, and I am not allowed to go and sleep in the barn with what about the rats and it would be too cold in winter and it is out of the question.

We hear the car drive away and it is just me and Jerry in the kitchen, even the dogs are gone.

You'll miss your sister, you will?

Why are you not dead I say in my head like I'm looking at him. He is clearing the plates and I wait for him to ask me to help so I can still say nothing and he will just have to have me saying nothing and won't be able to do anything about it. But he does not ask me, he is sipping at his tea and putting things in the sink. He always uses the same mug and Mum always gives him the same mug. Afor it was just a mug like the others but now it is like it is his though no one ever said this is Jerry's mug. I can take it for my place and no one says anything like that is Jerry's, but it feels like it is his even though it isn't and the next meal he always has it back again. Now he's drinking out of it and he has left it on the edge of the table. I can just go and push it off.

It breaks into two pieces on the floor. One piece still has a bit of tea in it, and tea has all gone into the matting all dark.

Jerry picks up the pieces, one in each hand.

Did you let fall the mug?

I stare at where it was on the ground and I blink at him. My blinks are talking to him all I want to say.

Don't worry about it, I'll say it was me and I'll get a new one. We won't let on to anyone.

He goes back to cleaning up. He holds out the hand towel to me.

Will you help me dry the dishes?

It is the hand towel not the dish towel and he doesn't know anything. He puts it down because I don't take it.

No problem, young lad, that's no problem.

When he is finished he says he is going out to wash down the van and he will be just outside so to give him a shout if I need anything.

Why don't you play a game with him? she says. I'm not going to fetch down the Connect 4 and say, will we have a game the two of us? and let him turn on his heel and walk off on me.

I know well he's only a child but I was growing fond of that mug.

The fort I built him is out there rusting; he never once went in it. She showed me the knife mark he put in the teddy bear as if there was something funny in it. He holds his nose going into the bathroom after me even if I was only in there brushing my teeth.

Every day I see him I say hello, and he ignores me, looks me up and down and says nothing. Every night I go down the corridor say goodnight to him and not once a reply.

I'll get the van clean now anyway, even if it'll be my fault the Connect 4 or the Monopoly or whatever the fuck it is didn't happen.

There he is, in behind the wall. I thought it was a rat or a fox or something in the corner of my eye. He moves quick when he wants to. Moving too fast is what gave him away. I'd better let on I didn't see him. Does he think putting his head out from behind the corner low down at the ground he won't be seen? Is that what he's at?

He knows he's spotted, comes out now casual with his shoulder against the stone, a knife in one hand and a bit of stick in the other.

Let him stand and watch, no point going near him.

He probably wants a go with the pressure washer. The noise off the compressor must have brought him out.

He won't ask though, he'll stand there itching, wanting to pull the trigger on the washer instead.

Let him.

I KEEP THE STORY FOLDED UP under my pillow and sometimes I take it out and read it. But it is like maybe it is just a story and nothing else. At school when Miss Kelly says did you write anything in the summer I say no and she says it is a pity. We have to write what we did in our holidays and I do all about living in a caravan, but it is not a proper story because it is about things that are happened, and all that might happen is we have to go back to live in Jerry's yard. And that does not come true so I don't know about stories. I think to write one to test but maybe this one is still working so I wait. I will not read it anymore because when I look at it is like it is silly and has no power maybe, maybe I am wasting its power.

Jerry does not like the dogs. When they are table-ish and stare at him, he doesn't look at them at all even to say no. He says they are pets and not working dogs like it is a bad thing, and he keeps Jessie out in the barn. Rosemary and Jasmin are not allowed to talk to her and I am not allowed to talk to her and she is on her own and it is cruel.

I say to Mum does Jerry need more remedy and she says she will see and I am a kind and considerate boy—she will ask him. She says when she makes more she will tell me and I can bring it to him. I smile but I cannot stop and she says you're a funny one sometimes and she does not know anything.

It used to be like she knew in my head and now she cannot see at all and it is dangerous maybe. She will be very angry if she finds out but she can't and my secrets will never be known.

I say why does he need more, why is he not cured, because I can ask all I want without her knowing she is so knowing nothing. She says some things are hard to budge but I am not to worry. It is okay, she is looking after him. Maybe it is hard to budge because it was half poison the first time. It will be even more hard to budge the next time, it will be more than half next time it will be the whole lot.

Jerry is not there in the morning at breakfast and at bedtime he is not there. But we leave the gate open for him and his clothes are on the line and his washing machine he has put in in the bathroom where it is ugly. He is there at the weekends when B is home especially on a Sunday and he stays with me when Mum brings B back. I stay close to watch him what he is doing because it is to keep an eye on him and how I will get him.

He washes the Dyna and he has a pressure washer and he does the garage door too. Even the concrete bit in front though it is nearly night. He cuts up the big bits of trunk and uses his headlights to see, I sit in the van where it is not dark and the lights in the dashboard glow. He splits the wood and goes back and forward round the side to load the pieces, he is all shadowy when he passes and I hear the clanking behind me and then he is back bending down and loading up and he squints in the big light. I can see him and he cannot see me.

I will not help and he does not ask me, sometimes othertimes he says throw me that spanner like when he was putting the washing machine in and there was the horsehair and all the heavy bits and pipe and all of that. He was his teeth gritted and said ha ha and chuckled and ticked his teeth when water started dripping, and isn't that a fine job I made of it, we may go back and start again, and he took it all to bits again and I thought we would never be finished and then we were but then it was time to clean up and time to bring everything back, and then where does your mother keep the mop till we clean up properly. And then it was on to the next job.

I try to stay awake listening for the engine to watch him come in at night but when you try to stay awake it is the one thing that sends you to sleep so that is impossible. Trying to keep your eyes open makes them close and closing them makes you sleep as sure as eggs are eggs.

I try to wake up early to keep an eye. I bang my head on the pillow six times and say six six six and think all six six six six six while I wait for sleep so that my head knows to wake up at six. He is up afor me in the morning and who knows what he could do. I have all the bad thoughts and I think I will not sleep because when you worry you cannot sleep. But the worry is too much and to stop I think of nothing but six and keep six in my head so to wake up.

It works but I do not hear him go and he must be earlier than that and maybe he does not sleep like he has special powers. Mum asleep can be in two places at once, maybe when he doesn't sleep that makes him stronger and that is why the poison didn't kill him. Maybe the story is trying to work but he has his own magic to protect him.

I will only find out by watching. But I have to sleep and in bed the sleep is so heavy and once you are asleep it is all you ever want and stopping is impossible. Sometimes in the dark there is red taillights and sometimes I can hear the sound of the engine but mostly I am asleep and wondering.

B wrote a letter to me. It is just for me, in the post that is never for me, like a birthday card and even is that feeling. It is my name on the outside envelope and I go running with it in my hand everywhere yelling whoops. Mum said can I read it but no it is all mine and she said that is fine and enjoy it, all smiling. I can write back if I want and put the stamp and address perfect. I run upstairs and shut the door.

It is full of words I don't understand like I knew it would. She always has words like a brilliant game to play. It has a line at the top. *Dear Brat* it says, then it goes down.

Before you take umbrage please learn that 'brat' is brother in Russian. Sometimes happy resonances can be found in the pages of learning. This is my Sunday Letter Home, there is scribbling throughout the room about me and heads laboriously bent. There is little to speak of really. This afternoon during Games (Hockey and all that entails) a donkey wandered onto the pitch and disrupted our sport. Who knows where it was coming from or from whence it came, but it provided great excitement for a spell.

There is all bits crossed out and I can't even see the letters it is just like coloured in and the page is nearly through the other side. It starts again under. *I hope you are looking after yourself and looking after Mum. I know you feel that living with the man you call Jerry is an imposition, but let's speak plainly lest there be any mistake. You will just have to deal with it.*

With great expectations has all one line to itself at the end.

And then under is *BE XXX*.

I do not understand everything especially *imposition*, but I know she understands about Jerry now and that I have to look after Mum and protect her. B is expecting that I deal with it. Greatly expecting. She does not know, but I am dealing with it. The next time I will up the dose and give him pure poison—it will be all blue but he will not look. He will follow the instructions I give and then he will be dead.

Part Two

Hallowe'en

The fire is lit and Mum has moved the reading lamp over so we can see what we're doing. Beside the sewing machine there are oval bits of newspaper cut out, like egg shapes but bigger and not as pointy. We have to pick what we want from piles of old clothes—not for wearing, for material. We can choose as many as we like.

There is my T-shirt from when I was small that I used to wear for being a cowboy. It's exciting a bit and I show B and she nods how she knows everything. She holds up a big one.

Look at this shirt, who do you think wore this?

It is like a bit my cowboy shirt but much bigger with a collar, it is huge and less red. B has one pinch of her fingers at each shoulder and I don't know.

That was your father's, there's no point in keeping it, the elbows are gone and look at the collar. We can use it for your costumes though.

Why didn't he take it with him? B is frowning and her bottom lip is out.

Mum uses the big scissors we aren't to touch from her sewing box. The sound they make is heavy and sharp. It's a close noise and dangerous, but lovely.

He left behind much more than this shirt, darling, now pick some more material.

We hunt in the heaps. There's some of B's dresses that were beyond repair and couldn't go to the tinkers. B says we should pick as many different colours as possible and look for patterns and all of that. It's like searching for the best old crockery bits in the garden in Devon, and when I find a good piece B is very pleased with me. Some bits I think are good she just shakes her head though, but I find one with flowers on it and she says well done that's perfect.

Mum tells us to get on with choosing. We have to find five more each and that will be enough and she'll say when supper is ready.

It is happening and I can hear it happening—Mum is doing a remedy. I can hear the tapping. I bet it is for Jerry and I tell B. B has another shirt in her hands which is stripy, there are golden buttons and she has them between her fingers. She shakes her head like I do not know anything and says he is not sick.

So why is he taking a remedy then?

She stops—she did not know, it is not everything she knows. She wants to but she will not ask me because always it is her that knows things not me. I tell her it's not always something you can see. And I don't say any more. I do not know any more but that he is always working and never stops but that is not bad that is being a hard worker and the best thing in the world, so it is confused. But I do not say I do not know, I say nothing. This is new—me being king and B not with any idea. She says that's fine by me but oh ho ho it is not fine at all, it is very far from fine. She goes to the clothes with her back to me and doesn't turn round.

It is all quiet and the taps from next door are going and it is happening again, the story has not gone. I can already see doing it in the garage. It is very clear and it is not me in the past it is me in the future like it is a memory but will be yet. The story is at work and there is nothing to stop it, it is happening right now and already. It is I can hear Mum calling when it is ready and saying here darling and I can see myself taking it. It is I can already feel it in my hand. It is stinging in my hand.

I go to put my face up close in B's and say sometimes it's things you can't see, but that doesn't mean it's not serious, that doesn't mean he might not be dying and dead very soon.

You're a liar. No one even said Mum's making that for him, it could be for anyone. I will ask and you will see.

I follow her because I want to hear and I want B to see me when she is wrong. She has dropped the shirt with the golden buttons so I take it and now it is me touching the buttons. They are real metal you can feel it and maybe even gold.

Mum does not look round when we come in, she is in mid-count and concentrating and sometimes she does not even know we are there. I put on the shirt and it is huge like a coat and my hands are inside the arms and they are long nearly to the ground. The shoulders stick out and are big. There is something in them to make them stay up and out in a shape like big muscles. I am maybe a pirate king. I have the shirt of all coloured stripes with yellow in between and with all gold buttons and big important shoulders.

We stand side by side to wait for Mum and she is only in the five hundreds so we will have to go all the way to one thousand. I am my eyes a little closed for I am king and my chin is a bit up because I have superpower thoughts. B looks at me like I am something the cat dragged in. She says you know that's a woman's shirt don't you and she is just jealous that it is mine now and that I have the army shoulders. I close my eyes more but not screwed up—just gently because I do not want to see her. Like that she is gone. I stand and wait and I do not even know she is there but I can hear her breathing like she is right and I am wrong. She will see and ha ha ha to her.

What do you two want? Mum is smiling, but I keep my mouth closed and just watch B now she is wrong for once.

Is that for Gearóid?

Even B is calling Jerry Gearóid now all the time. She can't say it properly like the way he does, Mum too says it different and they both sound stupid. It's a stupid name.

Yes it is, dear.

B's face is red now all blushing up her cheeks.

Sometimes it is things you can't see, I explain again but she will not look at me.

That's right, but it is nothing for you two to worry about.

Now B thinks she is right.

So it is not serious? He is not dying? It is not something that can kill him? She is repeating the questions lots to show me that I am wrong.

It can kill people.

Mum looks grim and B is even redder now, the reddest, and I have won completely.

But it won't kill Gearóid. He would never. Mum is shaking her head and it is like she is talking to herself. She is not sure, she can maybe sense that something is not right but she doesn't know what.

Can I bring him the remedy when it's finished?

B is looking at me now, I can feel her eyes on my face but I do not turn for her and she doesn't understand anything. It will kill him and he will be dealt with once and for all.

Yes, of course you can, but I have a long way to go yet. You two are very sweet to be concerned but I promise you that Gearóid will be fine, he is fine. Run along now.

It is all like I knew it was. I can hear Mum calling when it is ready. It is already happened and Mum knows. I saw her face and it looked like it was to be, not sad but angry as if she did not know where it had come from or how but he was sick not better and he was already gone.

In the morning Mum says it first thing. I am in the kitchen, like I knew it would be—here darling, and she is holding out the pot to me and I have it in my hand. It feels like I knew it would feel and the stinging comes that doesn't hurt and my whole body is like I am fizzing and it is what is holding me all together. I am I don't know where or when.

Mum says, Gearóid is out in the back field I think, why don't you bring him this and give him a hand? It's for the bonfire, that's a job you'll like.

Nobody knows anything and I am in the garage and the yellow gloves are big and cold in the fingers, wet but there is no water. My rubber yellow hands put the box on the ground. The spoon is inside and the powder is living blue.

I pour out nearly all the remedy—it makes a shining little pile beside. I flick it all away over the floor.

The careful spoonfuls go in the little pot and the spoon goes in the box. I clean the floor with splashing water and hide the gloves by the axe.

The chainmail is like a drowning skin, falling down heavy on the shoulders, close as neck hair, the taste of the metal like blood. Its weight on the back of the hands, the ends of the fingers catching under the nails. It's liquid, but heavy like a blue gansey that doesn't let in the rain, only closer, pressing all at once. My long shield is curved at the top but all the way down to the ground where it's pointed, and the sword is big but it swings as lightly as this rotten stick. The nose-guard of the helmet is uncomfortable, it's flat down squashing. My nose feels like it might have been bleeding, a rust of blood snot at the rims of the nostrils.

I am hunting him and he cannot hide, him backing up the Dyna to the little gate into the back field. He may be having a Dyna but he is big like that and cannot hide with all the noise it makes.

I am running and he sees me coming and waits for me with his hands on his hips.

Will we make the fire?

He takes two strawbales out of the back. There is rotten old fence posts and pallets too, an old door and all of that.

I hold him out the pot.

Mum says you can use water to swallow it this time—the quicker it goes into the stomach the faster it will take effect.

He puts it in his pocket, okay lad, and he kicks a stone under the gate to hold it open. I follow him across the field one bale in each of his hands.

And you have to take it five times a day, I talk to his back.

Okay lad, but he doesn't turn round. It is good because I cannot stop smiling.

He puts the bales down one on top of the other. I point at the pile of branches from the chestnut and ask, are we going to burn them?

We should wait until next year, it was only the springtime when they were cut and they'd be too green maybe.

He will be not here next year. But I say nothing at all just try not to smile.

We can try if you like, she was dead before she fell down, but don't be disappointed if they don't take.

Some of the wood is so rotten it crumbles and falls apart on the field. We lean everything up on the two bales and it is like I am helping. Jerry thinks I was running over to help. This is how clever the story is being, even when I wrote it I did not maybe think it was real or it was possible to come true but now I see how can it does.

When we have carried everything from the back of the van it is already a big pile.

You're not content to stop there I suppose? It's a mighty great fire you're after.

I nod and I smile and he nods too though he's not smiling. He clicks with his mouth and says ah yeah, ah yeah.

On the kitchen table Mum wets big potatoes and rolls them in salt so all the salt sticks and then she wraps them in tin foil and brings them in a basket.

Our cloaks are waiting hung from hooks. They come down to nearly the floor. All around are sewn on the ovals of blue and red and purple thatch, bright grass green and a sand yellow the same to Bettystown. Piebald ovals too, brown and white like dogs or ponies, all of them are the same size, large eggs. The material is heavy and within them is all the magic. To put them on you have to fit your head through, there's holes for the arms with loose sleeves coming down longer than our hands. The hoods are pointy. With her hood up and her hands by her sides I can just see B's nose and mouth and chin, and then her feet. I do the same and the hood droops down so you can only see the floor right in front of you.

B walks across the field slowly. With the grass I can't see her feet so the cloak is like she may be floating. The cone head is very still on top. I put my own hood up again, just the hem of her cloak to guide me.

These are our wizard cloaks and in the dusk the trees are soot.

We have tapers we made soaked in wax. B lets me light the match that lights her taper. She crawls into the opening to reach the paper and the straw, and the cloak goes empty—it looks like it has been stuffed in and she has disappeared.

But her feet come backwards and she climbs up straight. She looks out to me from under the hood.

The fire is lit now, let the night begin.

When she speaks the flame rises and the sound of straw whooshing goes up in milky smoke, like it's pouring but going up not down. The crackles and the heat make us step back, and Mum's hand comes down in front of us. Same to when we're in the car about to crash and she puts her arm down like a barrier because I am always in the middle of the seats talking and her arm can go across us both. The fire is wild and there's no flames just a bright roar rising, and above there's red sparks spitting only up.

Jerry's face is warm and glowing, his cheeks look greasy and his eyes are in the flame. He looks down to me but I look away before he sees me. I wonder did he take his remedy yet, is the poison working?

The dark gathers behind us and Jerry uses a pitchfork for branches that fall out, throwing them back in. He goes around in a circle and then sticks the fork in the ground and puts his hand over the top end of it. This is what a dead man's face sees.

We all stand and stare. There's nothing outside the light of the fire, not stars no moon so there's nothing but the flames. The heat is on my face and at the back of my cloak a cold wind—behind me I know the dark and there is everything afraid in it, waiting outside.

I warm my back and watch the black. I take two steps into it and already the heat of the fire is losing, the crackling is lighter. I take three steps more and there's only the night cold. I keep walking because I am not scared and I am as much as the things in the night.

When I look back I can see a big only space—in the centre of it a fire and two people standing beside. Between them the triangle shape of my wizard sister, the ovals gleaming on her buttermilk cloak. The shape spins slowly like a twirl that's coming to an end.

She calls my name. I start towards her, and when she calls a second time the grown-ups see me coming. Their faces come to shadow as they turn, I see the sharp lines of them and then nothing. I run a little, my legs away under my cloak and I jump among them, among them happy.

Jerry tends the fire, it is small now and I take up safe ends of branches and throw them in. Over the burnt edges of grass there is soft-feet ash.

The fire roars up again in the middle of the black burning branches. Below they are like under snakes, half burnt in cinder sections. B starts to dance in wooden dance. Her arms must be out because her cloak is into the shape of a bird and her legs must be straight and stepping up and sideways, her arms are lifting up one side and then another.

I holler the Red Indian holler with my four fingers flat to my mouth making the air go loud and out. I circle B then I circle the fire and then I jump the fire and the flames draft around my legs.

Mum dances that way she does to The Archers' music sometimes, holding her hands out like she has a partner and waltzing away one elbow out. I hear the jerky wireless music and taste the fire ash and smoke, and Jerry is dancing like Irish dancing but slower and softer his legs go roundy not trotting up and down. Grey spumes rise up as his shoes spot in the ash, and his toes tap with no sounds in among the patter of his feet.

When the wood in the fire is only white and embers and there's a big circle we search for the potatoes in the foil and find them hot and soft with our hands. Mum splits them with a knife and puts big chunks of butter on. Jerry pushes the ashes and black smokers in towards the middle of the little fire and we sit on the warm grey ground eating the potatoes, the butter and salt skins, in the flicking of the last little flames.

Tired, God but I'm tired. Once you stop is the problem, once you sit down for five minutes then it comes up on you. It has the time to catch up with you then.

I'm fine when I'm moving. Always onto the next job, building the fire, tending the fire, watching it to keep an eye on it, even dancing round it. There I was dancing a half an hour ago but now it feels like I may never stand up again. I can hardly keep my eyes open.

I'd sleep here only it would be cold when I woke. And what would they think of me sleeping? These people have taken me in. I was like a whipped pup, a dog lost out on the road a long time. And now here we are sitting on the warm ground together, a fat lot of good to them I'd be curled up in a ball and snoring.

I can only guard them when I'm awake.

Christmas

Mum scrapes and scrapes to clean the bowl and then uses the fork to clean the spoon. I keep thinking for her to stop but she keeps going not to miss a bit. But she can't get it all and there's always some left. B is watching too.

Give me some room for God's sake.

Mum puts the big round tin in the oven, the last splats of mix still lying on the top that haven't sunk in yet.

Now, who wants the lick?

Me me me me me me me me, mine, I do.

B stays silent but she doesn't let me push in front, she has knees and elbows all the time and the back of her head is very hard. Mum takes the spoon and fork in one hand and the bowl in the other and holds them up high, above grabbing.

Whose turn is it to choose first?

It's mine, says B. Last time he chose first, and took the bowl as always, and ended up sticking his head in it in his usual manner and you laughed because he got some mix on his nose as well as in his hair.

B is a liar and what's most unfair is that she gives her lies facts to make them true. Just because I can't remember why it's my turn doesn't mean it isn't. I kick her leg right at the front where it is all bone and really hurts. She always goes for the hair, but I get her by the wrists so she can't pull too much.

Stop it right now or I'll give it to the dogs.

The dogs are up and sniffing too so B lets go and I let go. She stands there doing that silent one-tear fake pretending and her face is red. My hair hurts where she pulled it—it's different pain to other things, it's way sorer.

Right, it's B's turn to choose first.

B can't help that little smile she has even though she's trying to keep her mouth all sad.

I cannot believe this. I think about the pain on my head and tears start for me too, loud and out.

Well I don't know but you kicked her, which was a very nasty thing to do. And, as she's just back, she can choose first as a welcome home. And—Mum is raising her voice louder to mine—if you don't stop shouting I'll let B have it all.

There's nothing to do so I stop, but I will have revenge. B gives me that side look and I hate her. She takes her time choosing from all the angles.

I'll have the spoon and fork, please. Thank you.

Now, she's even let you have the bowl. Isn't that kind of her?

B is sitting up, nibbling at the small scrape on the spoon handle, she's not even starting on all the really thick stuff on the edge or in between the fork bits. There's nothing in the bowl, but she's made it look like she was being nice.

When you two are finished that why don't we go and decorate the tree? I'll get the Christmas box down. Mum is away and down the corridor and the dogs following. It is only B sitting licking at the table.

It's a lovely Christmas tree that Gearóid brought isn't it?

No.

It's just the perfect height for the drawing-room ceiling—much bigger than the one we had last year.

I hate it.

How can you hate a tree?

Jerry bought it.

Yes, but what's that got to do with the tree? You need to grow up.

B's face is all pained like when she has to go back to school.

It's nice that Mum has someone, so that she is not on her own.

She has me and you.

You must try to think about other people, not just yourself. B twists her spoon all looking at it. Why don't you like him?

There's so many reasons and no one's asked me, so many that I can't even begin. I don't know what she is thinking because she said to deal with him and now it is all different. B liked her room and now they're in it. This is the best reason to start with.

He took your room.

B stands up. She takes the empty bowl and puts the fork and spoon inside. It was the wrong reason to give, she hasn't even said anything.

Come and do the drying up, she says. You must stop being mean and stupid. You're not upsetting him, you're upsetting Mum. I'm not asking you to like him just because we like him. I simply want you to behave a bit better. For Mum's sake.

I can't believe B says she likes him and how that has changed, but what does she know? She doesn't even live here properly anymore. The problem is that when B speaks to me and it's only us she always says the truth, apart from when she's lying to scare me, but that's not now.

Are we agreed?

Fine, I say, that's fine.

She grabs my shoulder so I have to look at her. I said are we agreed? Her thumb goes up against my bone.

Yes. Agreed.

B's eyes are putting holes in my head.

He will be dead soon anyway.

She crinkles up her eyebrows like what I am stupid.

What do you mean?

I shouldn't have said it, but she said for Mum's sake and maybe Mum will be upset when he is dead. B and her better get used to it.

Why did you say that?

I close my face and lift my shoulders up. B reaches out and takes my ear in her hand. She does not squeeze hard to hurt but it is held and she can twist and tear it. My head bends to the side and my neck.

Tell me why you said that.

I wrote it in a story.

Explain yourself.

I put in a story that I killed him and it will come true. The stories that I write—the things happen.

You wrote a story, and it is going to kill him?

She lets go of my ear and it is not often that she smiles a big smile but she is smiling one now, but it is to be mean and laughing like not real laughing. She shakes her head and she has stopped laughing so she makes up another same nasty laugh.

You're an idiot. You think things you write in stories happen in real life? You're stupider than I thought.

I am not stupid she is stupid, she doesn't know anything really just how to laugh like it is nasty.

It is happening. I am killing him and he will be dead. You said to.

Her eyes go together like it is one eye at me.

What do you mean?

There is a big empty space all around me where I can go anywhere but I am trapped because there is no bit to hide in.

Because in the story. And you said in the letter to deal with him.

No, what do you mean?

This time she has me by the throat—she is bigger than she was and even anyway I do not feel like fighting. But she is stronger than before and her nails dig in the tightness.

Tell. Me. What. You. Mean.

If I can just go back one minute then I can say nothing. I will not say he will be dead soon anyway when she looks at me and we are agreed and I can just stop and everything will be okay.

Last. Chance.

Mum will find out and she will be furious—she will send me away and she will not love me anymore.

You said to too, it is your fault too.

B turns her head and calls loud—Mum!

I put poison for the rats.

She lets me go. We listen for Mum coming and I start to cry a little bit, but there're no footsteps and no what is it, what do you want.

When Mum makes him a remedy I take the remedy out and I put the rat poison in.

When I say it out loud I know how bad it is, and B's face shows how bad it is. She is not saying anything, she is like she is scared and B is never scared for anything.

Her face is like the statues of heads on Easter Island, it is like she is toppled over but there is no moving her mind.

I have to tell.

You can't tell—I will stop—I have not done it. I will stop. It was just in the story and then it happened. I will stop.

All I want to do is stop, I will never do it again and I will burn the story in the fire and there will be no problem. But B is shaking her head even if she can see all my crying, and it is all over. But then I know what to say.

It will upset Mum if you tell, do you want Mum to be upset?

B knows I am bad for saying it and what I am doing, and even I have stopped crying, but it is the truth and B can always be got with the truth. I go back to crying but it is hard to keep going.

Stop crying. You need to answer me very carefully. Listen to me. Stop crying.

I suck the runny snot up my nose. It is difficult to breathe. But I have stopped, I know she will not tell.

Stop crying.

I cannot straighten my mouth, I try but it will not stay straight.

How many times have you done this?

Every time, apart from in the summer.

How much does he take?

He takes it five times a day and when he has none left Mum makes him more, and I put more in.

She is shaking and shaking her head.

There is no other way. Mum must hear of this.

I will stop! And he is not dead, he has been taking it all the time and he does not die, he is fine. He is not even sick. It doesn't do anything. It doesn't work. Mum will be so angry.

B is thinking. I know she will not tell. Please do not tell.

So why did you keep doing it if it doesn't do anything?

I fold my arms.

B folds her arms.

So you can just stop.

Yes, never, I promise. I promise!

But what if it has already made him sick inside and it will make him sick later?

He is fine, he is okay, he is not sick.

If he becomes ill even one little bit, I will have to tell right away.

I know. I promise.

I am only keeping my counsel because it will upset Mum, and Gearóid might withdraw his affections if he finds out what a horrible boy you are. You do not deserve any leeway, this is only to let others live in peace. It was a very, very stupid thing to do. You have to promise never—

I promise I promise—it was not me it was the story. I will put the story in the fire and it will go away.

Listen to me.

B sits on the floor and pulls me down so I am on her lap. It is a bit strange because she is not big as Mum and her arms do not go all the way round me properly, but she is holding me moving a bit side to side like in a cuddle. She is talking with her head behind my ear and I am not crying.

Stories are not real. It was you. You are in charge of you. Things that you do are you. Stories only happen in your head, if you stop it in your head the story will stop.

B's NOSE IS UP AGAINST THE glass and she is just staring out. The light from the candle is all worried on her face.

Why is Gearóid not back yet?

He's working, come on now you two, you have to get straight to sleep, it's late as it is. Father Christmas could be here any minute.

I wake up but I don't open my eyes. I'm sure I hear footsteps slow and heavy and I try to go as sleepy as I can because there's no way to pretend—and I do my best sleep impression. Not the one where you're showing you're awake and being funny, the one where you let your mouth go lower lip and you suck in the air slow with the back of your neck. And all the time I listen but there's no footsteps I was just thinking there were.

There's a weight on my ankles. I move my leg the smallest inch and there's a heavy weighing—I reach for the bedside light all wide awake, and at the foot of the bed is the stocking all sides full. The door is open and B is there, she's in her best nightie with the embroidery at the edges.

He was just here, get up, get up.

She's walking by my bed.

I know, I heard him too, his feet.

Why's your door closed? It's never closed!

She tugs it open and I follow. Down at the other end of the corridor—the door has just gone shut. We run and burst in to the black dark inside.

Mum and Jerry sit up in bed, they were deep asleep and they are confused. B has their bedside light on but Mum is finding it difficult to open her eyes and doesn't really know what we are saying.

What's that? What is it? Jerry is lifting himself up with elbows and yawning lots, and rubbing his eyes and stretching. Chilren? Hello chilren.

He was here, B's voice is she cannot believe it. He was here! We heard footsteps both of us heard footsteps and then we came out and we saw him come into your room—we saw the door close!

I saw his boot, I tell them.

Jerry and Mum look at each other and they are excited now too and their mouths open all the way. Jerry points at the far side of the room.

He must have gone up the chimney.

The fireplace is just beyond the shadow of light, we rush at it at once and lift our heads inside. There's only darkness and the smell of old stuck smoke. I can't see anything.

Shush, children, shush, be very quiet now, listen.

We don't move, silent in the soot black. I can hear only our breath, jerky, but we hold it to make it quiet. We listen so hard you can almost hear the listening, like watching the circles of a stone that's sunk under the water. There is only complete and ever never silence.

And then, far up the chimney, faint and away above outside, but clear and nothing else—a tinkle and a song chime in it, the sound of sleighbells ringing in the distance.

Church is full and everyone looks at everyone else. Jerry goes at the end of the pew and stands to one side like all the men to let the families in. All the people from every Sunday are staring but they have strangers with them too, and everyone is a bit odd looking, and clean jumpers and dark green suits. The stranger children are fat most of them and look about on slow pink necks. They are the same as their clean fat parents and I pity Mrs Parsons in particular she must be so embarrassed of them. I try to guess if it's her son or her daughter. None of them look like her and they are not in the least bit dignified. Some other people are in jeans, which is a disgrace, but perhaps they don't know any better. Jerry has blue trousers with a crease all the way up the front of each leg. He was polishing his shoes this morning, on newspaper on the kitchen table.

O Come, All Ye Faithful is the first one up on the board when I find the number and it's a good one. When the organ sounds everyone gets ready, one hand tucked under the armpit the other holding the hymnal open at hymn number 64, and then the whole church starts to mumble along together.

When the last one's ended there's not long left before it's all over. All the adults queue up and as soon as it goes a bit short new people join on the back. With the big golden cup bigger than her head, Mrs Tyrell gives them all a drink and then she finishes the rest with one gulp at the end.

Mum and Jerry don't go up. Mum won't tell me why not, she never does, and I'm to be quiet now. B whispers it's because they're living in sin, but Mum never went so it can't be from Jerry this time. Then B says as loud as talking, which is so loud after whispering, that I should think about what I have done and pray. Heads turn everywhere from the pew in front and look down and it is like maybe everyone heard. But Jerry is sitting back with his ankles crossed under the bench and Mum stays kneeling.

I close my eyes so shut I can imagine it away. But it is like everyone knows what I did with the poison now B knows, even if they do not know. And it was wrong and bad and maybe he will still be dead. I open my eyes because it is too scary with them shut and I see the plaques on the wall for people dead in wars and see what rank they were and all of that. When they have the same name they might have been brothers or even fathers and sons. And they are all dead and it is real and I do not want to kill someone, and not even Jerry. I am sorry and I pray and pray to make it go away.

The peace be with yous are my favourite when everyone turns backwards and forwards and we all have to shake hands. I shake all the hands I can get as hard as I can. It means it really is nearly over, though even the letting out takes ages. The priest stands in the hall by the big ropes for the bells and the flowers, and everyone has to go out by him, and shake hands with him and some people even stop and talk, which makes things even longer.

He smiles and smiles and smiles and his eyebrows go up and down and up. When it gets near my turn, close to the door and there's enough space, I run for it. He makes a ho ho chuckle after me like he allowed me out but he knows he lost and I'm away down the path among the gravestones.

As soon as we're back I go see Mrs Lynch. I have a bag of conkers I saved for her because they are her favourite. I hold out the paper bag and say Happy Christmas Mrs Lynch, even if it is odd saying it out loud. Her two hands go to her mouth and then she holds them in a ball in front of her.

What's this you have for me?

I want to say it's just some conkers I saved up but no words come out. She opens the bag and lows her face right down to see in, then she reaches a hand in and I can hear the fingers in the chestnuts and feel the bag is moving. They have gone a bit dull, but it is impossible to keep them shiny.

Horse chestnuts. Now isn't that something? You're a great young lad. Come in and you can help me with my hamper.

Out on the table she has a big box made of all bendy sticks weaved like a basket but square. She's unpacking it—tins and jars and boxes all with FORTNUM & MASON written in black. The sticks creak when she reaches in and I stand on the chair to look.

Who gave you this?

It's full of curly stuff like straw or wood or paper but it's none of these.

I have a hamper comes to me from Piccadilly in London, every year.

It's like the barrel of sawdust with who know what prizes might be in it. I want to put both hands in, but I know not to, though it's so hard. I hold the edge. Mrs Lynch has to go up on her tippytoes a bit to reach and her arm stirs and pats and goes deeper in.

She examines each thing with her magnifying glass.

I wouldn't even know what some of these are. Blackberries in syrup if you please. Tea, a tin of Royal Blend tea. What's this next one? Cream of watercress soup. This hamper is better than the last one, I think. Look at this now, a plum pudding.

I know to wait for Mrs Lynch to say who's it from, but she's taking longer than usual and she gave an answer but it wasn't really and I can't wait.

Who gave you this, was it your son Michael and—and his wife?

I want always to ask her name but I'm not sure she has one.

Beautiful presents Michael used to get for me, you're right to think of him, and was he a rich man in London the way he might have been only for—

Her face goes dark and her eyebrows are black when they come together, all the grey disappears.

But you think those two nowadays would put their hand in their pocket for something like this? It's herself has control of the purse strings. I told her not to bother after the flimsy yoke she got me last year, and I told them this year I'd have my dinner on my own. There's no need for them to put themselves out to come for me.

Was it Father Christmas?

Mrs Lynch wipes her eyes and lifts the empty basket down from the table.

It's a long time since he was at this house. Wait, and I'll tell you. I've known Richard Pink since he was in short trousers, and he was always a very polite young man. The older Pink, the uncle, sent me a little something every year and the younger Pink is carrying on the same thing. I keep an eye on what goes on around and about and they're very grateful for it. Do you know what my favourite is now, out of all them?

The table is covered with all the tins and boxes and everything is fancy, with colours that look like in paintings or smart book covers and posh ideas. I put my hands on my hips the same as Mrs Lynch to try to look the same way so to see what she sees. I try to guess but it's a torture. I know my favourite, for sure it's the box of Icy Mints. But I don't know for her. It must be the chocolates too, everyone likes boxes of chocolates the best. But you never know with Mrs Lynch, maybe the tea or the plum pudding, she said about the plum pudding. Or maybe even the big orange tin, the Fine Biscuit Selection.

This bag of conkers—it's the only thing will keep the spiders away.

My face feels funny and I am smiling but trying not to. I am so happy that it is even like not to show being pleased with yourself. I can't look at Mrs Lynch but I know she is smiling. It is okay being pleased with yourself with Mrs Lynch.

She puts a hand on the Icy Mints and holds the box in the air in front of me.

Take this away with you.

She lifts it out of my reach.

But promise me one thing, don't share it with anyone, sure you won't.

Mum has the tin of Quality Street from under the tree and says if there's a big fight like last year she'll put the lid straight back on.

I have an idea, says Jerry and everyone looks at him like why would he be speaking, we always have Quality Street and it's nothing to do with him. But Mum hands him the tin anyway, and he lifts off the lid—he does something that is awful and amazing. He kneels down and turns the whole thing upside down on the carpet in front of the fire. The pile glitters with all the different Quality Street colours and I go for them but B holds me back. A triangle pale green one, that's a Noisette Triangle, has gone near the under of the sofa where the fringe is and I keep my eye on it while I struggle. I'll kick it under further when no one is looking and come for it later if they're all somewhere else.

We'll divide them up into four piles, says Jerry.

He starts separating them but how will it be exactly the right amount in each pile and he's paying no attention to what flavours are going where. For once Mum and B are on my side and he says fine, okay, we'll each make our own pile and pick one by one.

This is getting good, and square is fair. As we all get in position on the carpet, I push the triangle one more under the sofa with the back of my foot too.

I get to choose first because I'm the youngest so it's Strawberry Cream of course there's no need even to think about it, it'll be Strawberry Cream every time until they're all gone. There are lots of the Peanut Cracknels—they are blue and have a nasty shape like a pooh but that has been baked in a bread tin, but inside is a hardboiled sweet even though they are covered in chocolate, which is like a joke that isn't funny, and they are peanut flavour—Jerry takes a Peanut Cracknel on his go every time. It's difficult to believe how stupid he is.

When all the piles are fair Jerry takes out the cards.

Who knows how to play poker? We'll play for the sweets.

He explains how we can eat as many as we like but the more you eat the less you'll have to bet with and the less you have to bet with the less chance you'll have of winning other people's. I look at B's pile and she looks at mine and we look at each other and grin. I'm going to win them all and I laugh out loud before I know what is funny.

The game is very complicated, and there's all combinations and even one that has no order but is all the one clubs or diamonds or hearts or spades called a blue. Jerry writes them down in a list and in the order of what is better than what else even though it doesn't seem okay three of a kind being better than two pair. His writing is like he holds the pen heavy and it is all in capitals. We have to do lots of practice rounds with matchsticks because someone has to open and they have to have a pair of jacks or better. And you have to always be able to show your openers at the end and twos are wild. You can change up to three of your cards once too, but Jerry is always asking who's shy at the start because you have to pay in to get cards in the first place, even if they are bad. But you're allowed lie and pretend you have good cards and as long as everyone believes you, you'll win. This is the best thing but it is not easy.

We play for real and I only eat one Strawberry Cream because I can't help it but no one else eats any at all so I don't either. When B gets Peanut Cracknel ones in her pile she swaps them with Jerry for nicer ones—she even got a Toffee Penny, which is her second favourite, for a Peanut Cracknel. Jerry says he will swap with me if I want but I don't want. When I get Peanut Cracknels I just use them first for betting. I don't need him for getting rid of them.

B is winning and then I am winning a lot because I had a blue and Mum goes out first and Jerry says don't worry you can share my sweeties and they laugh and it's not funny the way when you stub your toe isn't funny. And then I beat B with bluffing and I don't even have to show her my cards.

Jerry gives her sweets from his pile to eat, which isn't fair but it's Christmas and maybe I better give him some peace and quiet because what if he is dead because of me. And on Christmas. He is not, he won't, and it is only because B found out. Nothing is different to before and there is never anything wrong with him. I keep to my game and winning, but I look at Jerry to see he is not dying and he is fine. He is fine.

I am very careful and I pretend to bluff when I'm not really but Jerry knows because I only took two cards and then I think he's bluffing but he's not and I bluff and he catches me and I only have my best sweets left and they just go with paying in and all of that.

Jerry has all the sweets in a big pile in front of him and I won't cry, but the feeling to cry is very, very strong. Only the feeling not to cry is stronger.

I'm going to give these to your mammy and they are all hers now, says Jerry. And Mum says, now, who would like some of my sweets? If you ask politely I'll share them.

I think of when I had nearly all of them and I should have just eaten as many as possible, but Mum will be fair with her sweets, not like Jerry only giving some to B, so it's okay in the end. Even if I lost it was good to play—it is fair in the end with Mum giving hers to everyone. And Jerry says, no thanks no thanks let the chilren have them.

Imagine not having chocolates when you are allowed, he must want them really but is letting us have them.

Jerry is smiling watching B gobbling sweets even if some were his.

I don't open any even with my whole pile in front. I only had one Strawberry Cream before but I can taste it again in my throat. It is sharp like sick and the black chocolate is back sticking at the root of my tongue. Jerry would be sad if he knew I tried to kill him. I swallow and swallow but it will not go. I cannot take the taste away.

B separates her wrappers so there is the see-through plastic squares and squares of foil.

Jerry is on the sofa with his arm round Mum and I think of the Noisette Triangle that nobody knows about and will be all mine. And they are sitting above it and don't know anything. Jerry says *go mbeirimíd beo ar an am seo arís.* He's always saying things we don't understand and loves B and Mum asking him to explain.

It makes me sad but Mum is happy and sometimes it is okay if Mum is happy but I am sad at the same time. I can be happy if she is sad so it is okay too.

B is careful putting the kettle to boil and the way that girl lays out the spoons on the tray you'd swear she was handling surgical knives. I go for the milk.

–Jug, she says when she hears the fridge door open.

The small size of her; two hands to guide the milk and the frown when she pours it.

All the jobs done, she sits up at the table and puts one hand on top of the other and sighs.

– A watched pot never boils.

– Indeed it doesn't, baineann faire bruth de phota. *Will we go back inside?*

– Where are your parents this Christmas?

It makes me laugh the directness of it, and maybe she's only making conversation to pass the time.

– I hope it's not an indiscreet question. She has her eyebrows raised, but it's not clear whether she's worried about offending me or telling me off someway.

– No, that's OK. My mother is on the island and my father is dead.

– Do you miss him?

– It was long ago.

The little wince on her – and is it sympathy or the fact I didn't answer her question as straightforward as she wanted? The noise of the kettle makes things even quieter. We sit and listen to it rise.

– He was drowned.

The wince is held in her, she knows there's more to it than that. She can't help but be curious.

– I used to help my mother make him his lunch to take with him. It was my job do the tea. When I had it made I'd put it in

a jar, and then the jar would go into a big sock and that would keep it warm. I'd bring him out the sock of tea then before he left, that was my little job. So to answer your question: I do miss him, I suppose, I think of him every time I have a cup of tea.

Her eyes dart over to the kettle as it comes to the boil and she looks from it to me; huge alarm for a second until it shuts off with the click. I keep talking.

– They went out early in the morning some days, rowed over as far as the Cliffs of Moher, fished out below the cliffs there and were back in the evening time. And then one day they didn't come back. Two other men drowned with him.

She blushes, her big child cheeks, her face all red up to the roots of her hair. She's ashamed to have asked me, ashamed at what was discovered. I bring over the water, pour it into the pot.

– Don't worry, it's not a bad thing, it's just stayed in my mind that way with the tea. I'm glad I don't forget him.

She nods now and dares look at me again. She puts the lid on the pot. A busy sigh and checks left and right to see did we forget anything.

What was I doing saying that to a child? Upsetting her. I've no business putting that onto her. It just came out of me. God, now that I think of it, I never said those things to anyone before in my life.

– You carry the tray and I'll open the doors for you, she says.

On the fifth the decorations and all of that has to come down. If they're still up on the sixth, it's very bad luck. Bad luck like someone might die, bad even as if you hear a banshee. I did one night and Mum said it was only cats fighting but it wasn't, it was the sound of death coming for someone in a family, letting them know it was on the way. If there's anything left up, even a painted pine cone on the corner of a mantelpiece or a card on a windowsill it brings the badness. Taking down the tree and everything is easy, and putting away the decorations, but it's very simple to miss something small. Christmas is all well and good, but if there's a single bit of tinsel left out everything is ruined and it would have been better never to have lived.

We have to check everywhere, under the beds and behind the pictures. B finds a sprig of holly after we think we're finished and it's a big relief but if there was that there could be other things so we keep hunting.

I push back the sofa while they're upstairs double-checking the bedrooms. To eat the Noisette Triangle, I go corner, corner, corner then the middle. I'm careful the shiny pale green goes on the inside when I squash up the foil, so none of the Christmas colour can be seen, and I make sure all the chocolate is off my fingers licking. I bring the tight little ball of wrapping out to my bit of garden and use the trowel so as to plant it deep.

Spring 1990

There's a space above the big metal garage door that's flat, and that's where I aim. The garage door makes an awful noise, but I'm improving. The best is to catch it after if I hit it the right strength—too hard goes over my head and too soft it bounces first. Every time I catch it again that's a point—if I shorten my grip and hit it fast and catch it again it's a goal. Not catching it is a point for Galway and if I hit the door they score a goal.

The Dyna is coming, making more of a noise than usual, and I go for an injury-time goal but it flies over my head. He'll park right in the way as usual and sure enough he does. But pulling along behind is a big white trailer. There's orange on the bottom half and orange writing on the side. The word comes out loud—BURGERTHING.

Jerry opens the door at the back with a key, reaches in and takes out a wheel brace. He lowers a metal leg like a jack at the two back corners then unhitches the trailer and pulls the van away.

Mum's always trying to get me to ask Jerry things and it's stupid. Yesterday after supper we had bread and jam and I asked Mum to open the jar and she said ask Gearóid so I kept trying myself. I asked her again and she said I told you, ask Gearóid, and I put the jar in front of him. Jerry went to open it but Mum put her hand on it and said no I'm sorry Gearóid, this has got to stop. She always says I'm sorry when she's not in the least bit sorry. If he wants you to open the jar he has to ask you. Jerry wouldn't open it then and I just said I changed my mind I didn't want jam.

Jerry took it to have jam on his bread, so he could show me that he was having it and I wasn't. He doesn't usually even have jam, he has marmalade with horrible bits of peel in it. He was taking the jam to show off. But I won in the end because he wasn't thinking. When he opened the jar to get jam for him he didn't put the lid on properly after, and I just said I changed my mind again so I had jam in the end. Mum said, say thank you, but I didn't have to because I never asked him to open it.

I never ask him anything and I never will. He steps up into the burgerthing and a lid opens at the side a little. Then outside he lifts it up fully and fixes the bar to prop it. When he walks away down between the sheds towards the house and he's gone for sure I go to look in. There's all stainless steel, and a fridge and shelves, and everything is covered in like dust but not dry. It smells thick and a bit like butter that's turned.

Do you want to help me clean?

Jerry is standing beside me with cloths and a scrubbing brush and all of that.

I need some hot water. When the kettle is boiled will you bring it out to me?

He's acting like everything is normal and I don't want to ask, but I have to. I'm not really asking him, I'm just asking a question.

What's this?

Jerry climbs in and opens and shuts the fridge.

It's a trailer for selling burgers and chips out of. There isn't much money to be had in the sheep anymore so I have to think of different ways to earn the few bob. And this yoke will be just fine once she's cleaned up. Here, we'll take the fridge out of her and put it in the garage for now.

He waggles it out one way and another. When his head is ducked down and he's pulling at cables, I throw the ball out onto the toe of the hurl and I'm gone, running with burgers and chips in my head.

Jerry often stays out all night lambing and comes home for breakfast when I'm up getting ready for school. Mum is always saying, why don't you ask him about it if you want to know, and she will not tell me. She is, ask him, he'll tell you all about it, but I won't. I don't really care. Only that he does not die and what if the poison has damaged him inside and it is waiting for his death quick as a flash. If I have killed him it will be my fault forever.

When he comes in he leaves the door open and goes to the sink to wash, rubbing up to his elbows as if he's so good at washing his hands. He is always talking about the sheep so I don't have to ask anything, I go back to the porridge. I'm nearly through it. He's going to tell anyway now he's being given his bowl. He always has it full right up and he even licks the spoon he likes it so much. He would not be hungry like this if he was nearly dead.

Do you remember when you came in with the lamb this time last year?

Mum is smiling in a way I do not like and her head is on one side on purpose. It's right on her shoulder.

I do.

He is licking the spoon and he smiles back at her all twinkly eyes and he looks down at the table and up again.

That's nearly the last of them now, two more ewes and they aren't far off. I've done up the list for the cash-n-carry, if you have time today then we might be ready to go on Friday. No reason why not.

Would you not take a weekend off first? You haven't slept in a bed for two weeks.

He does that smile he does, and that up-nod that looks like a yes but means no.

Arra, he says and he reaches for the tea.

He has a new mug he brought, he uses it every time and I never touch it. Ever. I will clear the whole table for washing up but I always leave his mug, I will not touch it.

When Mum picks me up from school the car is full of bags of rubbish. We'll go to the dump in Mullingar first and then on to the cash-n-carry. Come on, hurry up, lots to do.

At the dump there's seagulls even though we're nowhere near the sea. There's diggers and a lot of noise and the smell is so strong it makes me almost sick, my throat comes up into my mouth. A man in a high-vis that has lost its glowing beckons us back as far as we can go then lets out a shout to stop that you can hear above the engines. We bring the bags up a hill of all rubbish and mud, up onto a ridge like a big stuck wave. There's track marks from the digger and it's best to walk on these because it's more solid. The seagulls aren't scared, they come so close they're huge. One eats from a nappy and picks it up and puts it down. There's crows too, but they stay out of the way of the seagulls. The gulls have yellow claws bigger than your hand, and hooks on their beaks like cormorants, and dinosaur eyes.

Tinkers come along the ridge, and the adults go to the boot of our car at the edge and look in. Two girls—one younger than me, one older than B—come to us on the rubbish hill. I think they will take the bags from out of our hands, knee-deep they come right up but then they stop. The little girl wipes her nose and the big one snatches back her hair and they wait, eyes on the bags not on us. We empty them out, all plastic washed out and folded up and Mum says there's nothing for you, I'm sorry.

They don't listen though, they bend among the rubbish as we tip it out and bits fly off in the wind. Mum folds the empty black bags under her arm as we go back to the car.

I'm sorry she calls, I'm sorry. You really won't find anything worth your while, I assure you. The man and the woman standing by the boot believe her. They walk back up to the patch they had been at, where the arm of the digger jerks down to turn up more.

I cannot believe the cash-n-carry, it is the best thing ever. Trays and trays of Bacon Fries and Scampi Fries are the first thing I see, hung on the corner, and then down that bit all the kinds of crisps you can think of, huge boxes of Tayto and even Monster Munch. Mum says I can go and wander while she does the list—she has a big flat trolley with a sheet of ply on it and no sides. There's an aisle of only big boxes of chocolate bars, all covered in plastic like blocks built up in walls, another aisle of sweets, huge see-through bags of bags of sweets, towers of tubs five high. I can touch them, a lot of things are too heavy to lift even but I can push them this way and that. Mum comes and tells me to stop it. She looks at the list and takes three boxes from all beside each other—a dark blue Cadbury Snack, though it's a rip-off of the Jacob's Club that is yellow, and a yellow box of shortbread and a pink box of the wafer. She piles them one on the other and I sit on the trolley beside and off we go. I keep my arm on them to hide them a bit in case she changes her mind.

She stops by the drinks and there's rows and rows of bottles in six-packs like red lemonade and Cidona and below them whole pallets packed with row after row of cans. She picks up one whole chunk of Club Orange, one 7up and I can't believe my eyes, one of Coke, and stacks them the other side. Now I'm like in an armchair of the best things there is. I count them and there's twenty-four cans—four one way, six the other. They sit in a white cardboard tray and the whole thing is wrapped in plastic. I put my finger on the plastic bit in between the tops of the cans where there's space. If I press down far enough it goes through. I do another one, and then another one. I can feel the smooth side of the can with the tip of my finger.

Mum starts shouting so I stop. I didn't mean to do so many holes. She takes a huge box of burger buns and then five litres of ketchup, a whole bucket of mayonnaise. There's big plastic tubes but they're actually more expensive so we go with the other ones, only the mustard we get in the tube. There's a big round tub of curry powder for curry sauce and I say yuck and Mum says I know, darling, I know.

For a huge tin drum of sunflower oil Mum has to use two hands. The metal is the golden colour same as oil is, and it makes a slop boing noise as she hefts it down.

We get bundles of brown bags, and thin burger bags, and stacks of white punnets, and foil trays with the white lids stuck to the side under the plastic sheet. I have to get off the trolley for the next bit. At the back there's a freezer so big it is like a room, it has a door and long flaps and ice steam comes out. I am scared when Mum goes in with the man in the white coat but she comes out soon with him behind piled with boxes. She's carrying big white bags with pictures of yellow chips on the front, one on top of the other so they come to under her chin. The boxes are smoking cold burger patties, chicken burgers, quarter-pounders, the names in black on stickers when you look close. We have to hurry now otherwise everything will defrost. We run in a trot to the paying place and they don't even take it off the trolley, the woman just comes with the beeper and looks with her head one way and then another and counts with her finger. Her tongue is out of her mouth and her big eyes are slow and she counts everything again a second time. Mum comes close to my ear and says don't stare very quietly, but why not stare? I'm just looking.

I've never seen so much money in my life as Mum takes out of her purse—twenty after twenty after twenty, all big and lilac blue. She counts it and the woman counts it and then there's change.

And five and three and fifty makes ten says the woman, sounding very pleased, which doesn't make any sense but Mum says perfect, thank you very much and doesn't want me asking questions right now.

A man helps us lift it all into the car and we drive away. I still cannot believe it really and I keep my eye on the building as long as possible.

Can anyone go there?

No you have to have a card—we're borrowing one for now but we'll have our own in due course.

And then we can go whenever we want?

Yes we can.

And if I save up I can buy things there too?

Yes, if you like.

I begin to think of what I'll buy, but I will have lots of time to make up my mind while I'm saving.

Can we bring B next time?

If we go during half term we can.

Even B will not believe that place, the place where shops go to the shops.

Jerry has pushed and pulled a big chest freezer in the garage and we put the frozen things in straight away when we get home. We stack everything else on cardboard beside and when it's done Mum tells a spell over it under her breath.

This is going to go well, she says.

In the corner behind the bikes is where the rat poison is and the spoon and the yellow gloves. I want to stop looking but I cannot. I can see just the shape of the axe under the sheet and I can't swallow. Mum will follow my eyes or I will fall down because I want to swallow and I cannot. I am sorry and it is all there is, I'm sorry, and there is nothing I can do.

Come on, she says and she holds out her hand.

On Friday Jerry is back early. It's only just gone dark when I hear the van. He doesn't come in so I go out to see. I run from the outside kitchen light, through the dark bit between the sheds, down towards the light from the garage open. Jerry has a big lamp rigged up with an extension lead. It's on top of a pole welded onto the middle of the metal bit of a car wheel, and it is too bright to look at. I go and stand in the garage entrance to not be in the way.

He is hitching the burgerthing onto the back of the Dyna. He has to back up and climb out and run to check the front of the trailer and go back in and reverse a bit more. I wave him back and point left a bit and say come to me come to me, whoa now go easy now easy.

I don't know if he can hear me over the engine. He jumps out to check anyway but says thanks lad thanks lad, you're a great young man.

He gets a light on and inside the burgerthing is all yellowy clean and spick and span not the way it was at all. He goes backwards and forwards, carrying in boxes and the cans and all of that. He lifts them in the door and then shoves them in on the floor under the counters, he puts the big box of Easi Singles in the fridge and the milk. The floor is all covered with everything. I help carry out the Snack shortcake in the yellow box and the wafers in the pink box and the blue box of rip-off Clubs.

You're heading up the confectionary department you are he asks me and he puts his hands on his hips. Now what am I forgetting? I have water, the jenny is in the van. I have my float.

Jerry scratches at the back of his head and holds his hand there. He doesn't move for a long time then he reaches in and turns off the light and locks the door.

Now a quick wash and I'm away he says, but he's talking to himself. He turns off the engine in the cab and goes to unplug everything. He loops up the lead up into the garage and comes back for the lamp rolling along its edge. I stay near him when he goes to do the garage switch because it will be all dark then. He pulls down the door and we walk together towards the outside light from the kitchen.

He doesn't want to eat anything but Mum says she'll put the kettle on while he washes and he'll have something before he goes and so he says okay then mam, because that's what he calls Mum sometimes when she is saying what to do.

She has bread out on the table and is hurrying with butter and the teapot. By the time everything is ready Jerry is sitting down and I'm having bread and jam and he's having bread and marmalade.

Are you all set she says, and he nods and chews and says I think so love, I think so.

Can I go with him, please Mum? I say, and I don't know why I've said it, but I keep thinking of burgers and chips and I helped do the sign that said MINERALS OR TEA/COFFEE 50P and inside the back of the burgerthing looked so exciting.

She doesn't say anything but I know she's heard me because I had to be brave to say it loud. She's looking at Jerry but he's clearing up breadcrumbs with his finger.

Maybe another time, she says after a while.

Jerry finishes his tea and wipes his mouth.

I don't mind if you don't, mam. It's not a problem for me.

Mum looks like she will say no, I stay quiet, telling her say yes say yes say yes under my head but she won't say yes, I know she won't.

Fine, well, if you really want to, I suppose it's no bad thing. But it's not up to me. If you want to go with Gearóid, you'll have to ask him yourself.

I jump up and I'm like a soccer player that's just scored a goal but I don't let it show. I know Mum thinks she's won getting me to ask Jerry for something but who cares about that.

Jerry is at the door, pulling on his boots. I go up to him before he goes and think if I need to bring anything but I'm ready just like this. I have my knife in my pocket.

Can I come working with you?

He nods once.

You're more than welcome to young lad, you're more than welcome.

There's only the sound of our steps together, his quick small ones keeping up alongside mine. I'm glad it's dark out here: it wouldn't do for him to see me smiling.

What jobs will he be able for? What can I give him to do that he can manage on his own? Better keep him away from the deep-fat fryer, it wouldn't do to have him injure himself. He'll be well able to get the minerals out of the fridge for people. Could he count out the money, maybe? The main thing is to keep him safe. I never imagined having a child to look after – maybe one day, is all I ever thought – but now it's here all of a sudden.

Those little steps are so light on the ground, but there's an awful weight to them all the same.

There's shearing blades on newspaper in the bottom oven now, rows of them, but the door is open like for lambs when it was lambing. Some even died and we'd dig holes for burying in the back field where the Jacobs could keep an eye on them. If B was home she'd make us have a funeral and she would say I'll officiate proceedings. Jerry would have to come as well. She would wear a sheet and a grey shirt from her school with a bit of cardboard cut out for the dog collar. We'd have to pray and all of that and B would go, now if you'd all like to turn to number 72 or whatever in your church hymnals, and we'd have to sing a hymn. She'd speak about the cycles of life and death, and life everlasting and death everlasting, and put snowdrops or a daffodil in before the earth covered the body. Ashes to ashes and dust to dust.

But if B was away Mum'd just be in charge—she'd go and talk to the Jacobs first, and make sure they were okay with looking after the spirit of the dead lamb. Then we'd put it in the hole and that would be that and there wasn't to be any fuss, we'd just have to get on with things. It would be Jerry that shovelled the pile of soil in on top. He looked very sad when he did it. I am worried sometimes all the time about what if we have to go and put him in the ground because it is my fault he is dead and he is ashes to ashes.

Now there're no more lambs but it is the blades of the clippers for shearing. They cannot be allowed to rust so they have to go in the oven to be sure they are dry after they are cleaned. I am not to touch them at all, but I can look in. The paper is either the Farmers Journal or the Meath Chronicle. If it is the front page it is best—I like *Meath Chronicle* more because the name is in the best writing, it is a bit swirly and important-looking, not like the Farmers Journal.

The blades are in rows because they cannot be in a pile, they all have to be separate. It is like baking when it is all cat's tongues only these are metal and look like crowns but flat. Jerry says they are very sharp but it doesn't look like it, I don't see how they cut. It is like lots of little scissors when they cross over and back but I do not see. If there is no one in the kitchen sometimes I reach in and touch one. They are pointy not sharp and the metal is warm.

I go with Mum to pick B up on Saturdays. It's important I get used to the place a little bit if I'm to go there. Mum says it isn't until the autumn when I ask, and yes I have to, that is the deal with Granny and Grandfather England and the Pinks and all of that. But it is not for a long time and I am not to worry about it now.

There is a huge gateway made with stone, but flat and grey and a long drive with lots of bumps in it. The big strange bushes all the way up it are called rhododendrons and Mum always says aren't they just magnificent, but their leaves look dangerous to me and the stems are twisted like evil trees. Then round the corner is the biggest house ever. We don't have to get out of the car, all the boys and girls are waiting on a grass circle. They are in the blazers and we drive round and when B sees our car she comes and gets in. The house is all dark grey and square and the windows are all the same size but for the ones at the top that are smaller, and the roof is the same grey and all the chimney stacks too. It looks like a prison. B says how little you know and Mum says don't be silly.

On Sunday, if I want to go shearing I have to be up before it's light. B doesn't want to come but all she does is read all day anyway so I go with Jerry. Mum wakes me and I have my porridge on my own because Mum is out with Jerry cleaning up the burgerthing from Saturday night. Jerry comes in, he has not slept since being out all night in Athboy and he has to have a shower to get clean. He says good afternoon young lad even though he knows it is the opposite. That is him codding.

I'm never really hungry and often I am not finished by the time Jerry sits beside me for his porridge. Jerry says come on, get it into you, we have to go working now. His hair is wet and not properly dry, he says the cold water is as good as hours asleep in the bed. We have to get going.

We're gone, mam, he says. He says that when we are still there. He means we are just about going to go. But we haven't gone, we are still there. We scoop up the last bits of porridge in our bowls, I have to race to finish even though I have been sitting at the table for ages and he is just there.

We arrive when it's getting fully light and sometimes things are well set up and the shed is ready and sometimes they're not and we have to help with gates and all of that. Sometimes the sheep are not even in, would you believe it. Jerry cannot for the life of him understand how people can be so badly organised, and would you look at the state of the yard. We put out the mats and I'm always trying to help but getting there just too late. Jerry moves very fast and he knows where things are because he was often there the year before.

Did you move the electric, you did? And the man says no and for a second they are both just standing still looking at one another and then it is hold on now a second while I think about it, do you know what, you're right, it was on that wall and I changed it when I got the compressor. You have a better memory than I have. And Jerry nods and nods, and says well will you let on where the feckin yoke is now, or do you want me to go hunting for it? And they both laugh but Jerry is moving again. I'm always following after him and seeing what needs to be done just when it is finished, just after Jerry has lifted the thing I knew needed lifting or fed out the extension cable when I am about to do it. But he keeps saying good lad, good lad.

At the end he gets his pampooties on and then he's ready. And when we get going I actually am help. I fold the fleeces when they come off and stuff them in the great big bags. You have to fold them right, but it's easy when you get the hang of it, though it's not nice when they're shitty behind and it's stuck to the wool. The smell is a bit like pee but different and the oil in the wool soaks in, and the wool is yellow close up, all into your hands and arms without noticing—but once you're used to it you know that there'd be nothing warmer than a fleece like that with all the stickiness in it.

It's impossible on my own to keep up with Jerry, he never takes a break and the fleeces pile up. There's always people to help though, there's often children sometimes older and sometimes younger and you can see in their faces the face of the man who owns the sheep. They look the same and walk the same. They spit if he spits sometimes, through the teeth. Once a farmer kicked a sheep right in the face and Jerry didn't see because he never stops shearing. He is always bent at the waist or spinning a sheep round—he says going gentle with them is the best, they only struggle when they're scared.

One escaped and there were shouts and I jumped on it and bounced off and everyone roared laughing at me and

Jerry had his hands on his knees and went red with laughing and choking too. He said once they're gone they're gone, you'll have no luck jumping on a sheep.

He doesn't ever stop long, every sheep is money, you get so much per head. Sometimes he'll drink water from an old 7up bottle and drink nearly the whole thing in one go. We go in for lunch most places. It smells weird in all the different kitchens, every one has a smell you've never smelt before. And the best is cabbage and bacon with white sauce and the worst is Easi Singles on soda bread. It is always the mother that cooks and sometimes the man and the boys are different when we go in to eat lunch and taking their jumpers off and quiet and helping at the table, and sometimes they are the same as what they were in the yard and the woman is mean-looking. Sometimes no one says anything the whole time and you can hear the plates and knives and forks, but there's lots of chat most places and Jerry pretends he doesn't know.

Where's little baby Deirdre? I was here last year and there was a little baby called Deirdre. Who's this young lady helping her mammy? And where has the baby Deirdre gone away to? The little girl will go all red, her whole face red, even her forehead, and she will be giggling and giggling and her parents and brothers will be looking at her and all laughing and she will be saying it's me, it's me and Jerry will be saying not at all, I don't believe you.

I don't look at anyone, I just eat and I know not to say yes when it is time for more even if it is apple pie. If you are allowed more they will put it on your plate when you say no thank you no thank you, and then it is go on and Jerry will say he will and I will have more and oh the custard too, lots of that. If there's not much Jerry will say he's enough. I sit beside him and he can hold out my plate for more or put his hand over it to stop them. There is always tea but no sheep will be shorn sitting in in the kitchen. We help with the plates though it's usually leave them there, I'll look after them. I say thank you to the woman and often it's the only time I have to speak at all.

We go from the strange kitchen that always smells different, and out to the yard and the shed that always smells the same everywhere.

It's a mistake to eat almost, the work is slower afterwards. It isn't slower though, that's just what Jerry says—it is still one sheep after another out the gate and spun round sitting and the wool coming off in one bit, like peeling a satsuma and having the skin all in one go. When he was younger Jerry used go to the All-Ireland where they have a competition for how many you can do in a day. That was when he was working with lads from Australia, lads from New Zealand, Māori lads even, the whole lot. They come from all the way round the world to go shearing and they might never really see outside of a sheep shed. And at the end of the season they're away to go shearing upside down back home. And they mightn't even see the outside of a sheep shed there either. They were workers and it was good. When there's two of you working you want to keep up with each other, do better maybe, and that leaves no room for slacking. He doesn't have time for the competition now though, he'd rather get paid. And he doesn't team up with anyone either, he's able to work just fine on his own.

On the drive home Jerry pushes Tom Petty and the Heartbreakers into the cassette player. He turns it up on loud and taps the steering wheel. The trailer comes clattering behind us and we eat up the road all the way home.

We shear the Jacobs at the end of the season when there's not a lot of shearing left to be done, and there's as much work with the two of them as there is with four hundred Texels below in Lally's.

Just catching them is job enough as they aren't in any way biddable.

There's lamb in the freezer, and I helped cut up a hogget from the year before. It had no head or feet and I held it with keeping pressure on it while Jerry went down the backbone with the big hacksaw. The marrow came out like toothpaste if you stood on the tube. There's a big cleaver and knifes so sharp I wasn't allowed near them, the next time maybe.

Summer

When the Pinks come we go to Jerry's caravan again. We're like sardines in a can and there's an awful smell of damp because there's been no one in it this long time. It's not the best and Jerry says he's sorry he's no place better for us to go. At night we hear them whispering and we'll all move in together someplace, next spring maybe. The burgerthing is going well and we've that bit aside.

Jerry says we'll go out west. That's the thing with a caravan is that you just hitch it up and away you go. It hasn't been anywhere for a long time and it's not good to have it just sitting in one place.

B and Mum travel in the caravan where B can keep reading and Mum can sew, she has a lot to do with my name tapes in all the clothes I have for going to school with B. There's a pile of grey shirts one on top of the other. School is not for ages and we have the whole summer yet, this is only the start.

I ride up front with Jerry. In the stagecoaches the man who wasn't driving had the shotgun and he had to keep a sharp lookout. Only for him the whole thing was a no-go altogether. I keep an eye on the map after Kinnegad, we go through places one after the other and I can see them coming—Milltownpass, Rochfortbridge, Tyrrellspass, Kilbeggan. In Kilbeggan we stop for 99s because we've been a long way, but we're only starting really.

We cross the Shannon in Athlone, the biggest river you've ever seen, three or four times as big as the Boyne and dangerous looking. It goes on and on for miles and miles and through lakes and out the other side before adding itself into the Atlantic Ocean. Once we are over the bridge, we're in the west and this is it.

We won't stop in Ballinasloe because it's bandit country, and in Aughrim there was a battle but we're not allowed to see because it is over this long time and there's only a field there now. Jerry may be wrong but it was Patrick Sarsfield he thinks, and he lost and went to France with the wild geese. I remember the pictures in the book with Miss Kelly of Sarsfield in a big hat and the story of how he won at Limerick with the raiding. I know Jerry is wrong about him losing. He says there's battles and there's wars, and you can win one and still lose the other. But that's just being clever. Anyway, it's only a field now the same as any other. They probably make hay in it.

When we get away out past Galway everything changes. I ask to stop to climb the rocks every five minutes and I say please and please every time I see some good ones, which is all the time, but it's not easy find a place to pull up. I beg beg beg beg beg until it's we might risk it here, and we pull in. B and me climb the rocks and Jerry and Mum come too.

We can see for a long way. B says it is beautiful and I want to walk out into it and across it, and Jerry says you want to go rambling and he knows what that is like.

Mum says the land is hard, imagine trying to live off it and Jerry agrees with her the way he always agrees with her. Me and B don't believe them, and Jerry says well do you see fields, do you see farms? And we do, there's nothing but fields, but Mum says they're not fields, look how wet the land is, you can't grow anything. Jerry says there's only B&Bs out here and that's a different type of farming altogether. Mum says the poor wretches and Jerry says to hell or to Connacht, but aren't we lucky to be living now. And Mum says yes, yes indeed, children you must always remember how very very lucky we are.

The Twelve Pins make you want only to go climbing and sometimes they're in cloud or the sun is on them, shining on the bare rock. The sky is strange round them, where they should be white the clouds are red and where it should be blue the sky is purple. There's no point trying to read there's only looking out the window, even B has left her book down.

❦

We stay in a caravan park with all other caravans but we only go there to sleep because it's full of people and none of us like people. We go out walking all day and climb up Errisbeg. Every time you think it is just this bit left it's only another ridge and you're never there. Even at the top maybe a rise you can see across the way might be a bit higher but never mind because look at that now, just look at that. The sun comes out again and lights across the lands and little lakes and silver streams far below—there's the shadows of clouds passing across the bogs and the green marsh ground that goes forever.

❦

We go to the beach and when it's crowded we go to other beaches, the best is places with no one there. We go in the ocean and run to get dry and warm up again. When it rains is perfect because everyone goes away and the water is warmer and we have a bar of chocolate to share.

If B screams *jump* we have to jump because otherwise we get hit on the back of the legs with the big seaweed sticks. Mum stands on the top of a sand dune and we have to climb up and she throws us down and says she's the king of the castle and we're the dirty rascals but while she's throwing one of us down the other can get up before getting thrown down too. It's a big dune but it's soft with the sand to fall on and we laugh until our stomachs hurt. There's shells and jellyfish and I find a dinosaur tooth but it turns out it's only a sheep's horn washed up. You wonder how it got out there in the first place.

JERRY SITS IN THE DOORWAY OF the caravan and he doesn't move. One time me and B go off for nearly a whole day walking and I even have to have a pooh in a field behind a stone wall. When we come back Jerry is still sitting in the same place. B says that's funny it's like you haven't moved since we left, and he looks up but it is as if he can't see us for a bit and Mum comes out and says can you two go and see if that place is still open for milk. When we look back Jerry has his face in his hands. My chest feels like it is tied with a rope too tight.

Mum says he doesn't like being away from the sheep and it's time we went back to them. But maybe it is the poison and he is about to die even right now. Maybe I will write a story where he lives for a long time, but B has explained the stories are not real so it will make no difference. It is all too late.

❧

Mum and B go back in the caravan again for the drive home, and Jerry puts Tom Petty on and he says sorry lad, and I don't know what he's sorry for. He says a man has to be useful, if he's not useful he's not anything.

I need to get back working that's all.

I think that I could have stayed forever in the mountains and on the beach. As we go away I look at the white lines dotting in the middle of the road and then all one and then dotting. They blur and they're clear and I was sneaking up around the sand dunes, watching the people leave the beach, and liking how long the dusk is and how like the water the air.

There was long sharp grass poking at my back. I was sitting watching the sea as the night began. The beach was empty and the bare rock bay ended like a bent-open horseshoe—it made a grey line that went out then all the way to the grey horizon beyond. It wasn't wet but it wasn't dry, there was a bit of a breeze and rain spotting. I don't know when I saw the black speck, but I watched it forever until it was a rubber dinghy coming into the bay. It came closer so slowly that it seemed to take always and no time at all. There was a man and a woman in the dinghy. He was rowing, and she was sitting facing him, her back to the land. It was a tiny thing in the grey empty bay.

They came straight down the middle of the water, and landed in the middle of the beach. Where the sand was hard they unloaded black bags and pulled the dinghy up from the little waves. They stood on the all around the edges and in the middle and folded it carefully, pressing and pushing until all the air was out and they could fit it into a bag.

The big dinghy was lying swollen on the sand, then it had completely disappeared. The paddles broke into little lengths and were packed away too.

I never saw a folding bicycle before, and I didn't think they even existed, but the man and the woman both began unfolding squares of metal, tightening the frames where they closed together, until two bikes with small wheels stood on the beach.

They helped each other attach the bags and as soon as they were finished, without looking at each other or back at the sea, they climbed on and cycled away.

I watched the empty beach and the empty bay, and out into the empty ocean beyond.

On Friday nights we go to Kilmessan and park up across the road from the pub.

The first thing to do is get the power on. The jenny looks a bit like a car engine, but in a steel frame. It's too big to go in the burgerthing and Jerry lifts it out of the back of the van. It's so heavy I can't even lift one side of it on my own, and he does the whole thing at once. We have a metal box for it to go over it too, with polystyrene all on the inside and a grill bit for air that has to be on the right way. People were complaining about the noise and it's true that it makes a racket all right. It's just all part of keeping out of the way of officialdom.

Kilmessan is always very quiet to begin with. Some people see the light and come too early and the oil isn't hot and they want to know why are you open then. Even if we leave the hatch closed they see the light and come knocking.

There's one or two people buy burgers and chips instead of making dinner, because it's the end of the week and why not. Women will pull up in a car and leave the engine running. After they order, they fold their arms and smoke a cigarette, leaning themselves back against the bonnet. They have enough done and feck it anyway.

And sometimes it is—is this your lad?

They think I am his son even and we just don't say anything because it would have to be explaining and all of that. Jerry just says he's a great young lad and we let them think what they want.

The chips are ready when they begin to float. I'm not allowed lift the basket out and shake it, or do the hooking it on to let the oil drops drip back into the fryer. But when Jerry dumps the chips into the big steel basin I can use the metal scoop. You fill a punnet and put it the right way up in the bottom of the brown bag, then you throw one scoop in on top. The size of the second one is how much you like the person. If it's mammies sometimes we even give them two second scoops and say this is your bag here, keep it away from the rest of them. When it's quiet you say salt and vinegar and they say lash it on, loads, or sometimes just salt if they're a bit thinking they're better than other people. Sometimes they even make a face and say I hate vinegar as if they are too good for it. My favourite is closing the top of the bag and shaking it after. Then you say there's ketchup, mustard or mayonnaise and they do that themselves because they know how much they want. If it's busy then they just look after themselves altogether. The salt is in the big tall Saxa tube with the red lid and we have malt vinegar with a hole in the lid from the small Phillips. After dinner time and before the pub shuts there's nobody for hours. Then everybody comes at once. It'd be easier for us if they didn't but that's not the way it works. People always do the same thing as other people.

We get everything ready for the rush. Jerry gets the patties cooked and keeping warm stacked on the side of the hotplate and he chops the big Spanish onions to get them cooked too. I get the bags in order and make sure we have everything we need ready to go and accessible in the fridge. Accessible is when you can reach things without having to move other things. I have a chicken burger with mayonnaise and as many chips as I want to eat and I have a can of Club Orange. There's a shadow of light in front of the burgerthing and then it's all dark and the only other is the green and yellow front of the pub across the road and the sound of the jenny.

I bring a book to read or we practise adding up the prices and giving change. When we do it for real Jerry says how much it is but I can take the money and do the change—it's easy, you have to do very little maths, just count up from the amount. And then count it into the hand to re-check, and do it out loud so they can see they're getting the right money. The thing to remember is always keep the note you've been given in your other hand. If you put away a fiver they can say it was a tenner they gave you. It happened to Jerry once in Athboy and it won't ever happen again.

I used to be a bit scared when the people came out all together, mostly men, and their voices are loud because one or two of them have a little drink taken. Jerry will call out to them, well lads and the brave few lassies, and he lowers the two baskets full of chips into the oil. As the orders come in, he puts the buns out on the hotplate to warm and spreads out the patties and mixes the onions. He says, up the airy mountain and down the rushy glen. And he looks out to see if anyone has the next line.

We daren't go a-hunting for fear of little men. Do ye not remember your schooldays?

Some of them do of course, and they join in, by nowadays most of the crowd know it and they all say it like with Miss Kelly.

Wee folk, good folk, trooping all together—green jacket, red cap, and white owl's feather!

One night a man said louder and kept going, he knew the whole thing and no one said a word till he was finished. Even Jerry stopped with the burgers and put his knuckles on the counter and listened.

There was a bit about Brigid and it was sad, and the man's voice nearly went out and there was a cough and one or two people moved maybe, but the man kept going and everyone went still again.

They all clapped when he was finished and Jerry said that man was to go first and he'd eat for free. And there was a few people saying ahh and no and all of that but Jerry said it was the same for anyone with a poem. And the man came up to the hatch and said the Brothers weren't all bad, the way they taught us one or two things along the way.

Some of them know Jerry from farming and they shout from near the edge of where the light goes out.

Hello, Jerry the sheep-shagger, do you be often shagging the sheep? Only in the springtime to see them right for summer, says he.

The word is shearing but they're only slurring their words. And they're to mind what they say because there's chilren present. They look at me pie-eyed and they agree, and some of them look a little sad sometimes.

Do you like trees, hey you, child, do you like trees? says a man in a council jacket shaking a second go of salt and vinegar into his bag. I'm not sure what the question means and I nod. He closes his eyes and nods too and it's like he's stopped thinking for a while, but we aren't finished talking.

I am polite to the customers.

Do you?

What?

Do you like trees?

He opens his eyes wide like someone has stood on his toes. No! They're all roots and malignancy—cunting fucking whoring yokes.

Jerry talks to them in Irish when they annoy him and sometimes Tommy says you may fuck off back to the fucking Burren or wherever the fuck it is you come from, you big ignorant.

Jerry makes him say sorry before he gives him the sausages as I'm only a young lad and shouldn't be hearing things like that. Tommy is my favourite and he's the only one to make Jerry smile when he doesn't want to. He always has a big chip and two sausages and I'm to horse on the salt, horse it on.

He was nearly knocked down by a car one night outside the pub and he stays talking and talking. He is last when everyone is gone and Jerry asks him has he no home to go to and he says not much of one now if I'm to be honest with you Jerry, but that's the way it is.

The poor man lost his wife last year and there's no one coming after him on the farm.

When everyone has gone that's when the work begins and it's the end of the night, it's even into the morning, so it feels like work should be over but it's the opposite. The deep-fat fryer is switched off and we go quick, as everything is easier to clean when it's still warm, and while we're at that the oil cools so it can go back in the drums for the next night. We have hot water from the Burco and when we've used the last of it the Burco sits down on the floor. We have to make sure everything is off the shelves. One night we forgot the cans and they were all dented and rolling around when we went to unload.

When everything is done and the light is unplugged and the trailer on, I wind up the jacks and put the wheel brace tucked in beside the fridge. It's the last thing to go in and then Jerry locks the door.

He shuts the jenny off and Kilmessan is swimming in quiet—you forget the steady plough sound of it until it's gone. The street lamps glow steady and everything else is asleep.

Every night I hope this is the end, when I watch him unplug the cable and loop it up, when he lifts the jenny into the Dyna and we back it up to hitch up the burgerthing. But it never is. He takes out an old fertiliser sack each and we go along the pavement and gather all the rubbish we can find so the people of the town have no complaints. People just throw the bags and cans and wrappers on the ground when they've finished, and sometimes they don't even finish—you see half burgers, whole things of chips and they're the worst to pick up when you get sauce on your hands or you're picking up cold chips. Jerry goes quick and far and comes back my side of the street and, even when we're finally away, if he sees any of our rubbish in the headlights—a punnet of chips with a red ketchup glittering—he'll pull up the brake and jump out after it.

When we get in, we unhitch the burgerthing and hitch up the shearing trailer, then Jerry tells me to go to bed, that I've done enough. He comes in to wash and change and I hear him go out again sometimes before I sleep because he has a long way to go often. He says he wouldn't sleep during the day and working at night is a lot better than lying snoring. I know what he means, it can be hard to sleep after all the work, and the smell of the chipper and the people are in your head and the grease in your hair.

My throat was dry from the heat and all the shit I'd been talking. I pulled out the stool, let the rest of the Burco out into a bucket for it to cool off a bit. Went for the milk from the fridge and I knew by how still he was standing he was at something. The finger out pointing at the cardboard sign he'd made: MINERALS OR TEA/ COFFEE 50P. *His eyebrow a fraction up, that way his sister has, that way his mother has.*

Smiling, the lids of his eyes half closed, being funny. Tapping the sign then on his tiptoes as if I didn't understand what he meant.

– I think I earned my tea already, I said to him.

I caught myself but it was too late, he'd noticed. The tone in my voice slipped that little bit. And the smile went from his face.

It was then I realised, when it was gone, that it was the first smile I ever got off him. He was only joking with me the poor craythur, and I wondered would I ever get another smile out of him.

Now every time I switch off the hot plate and the chip oil, he jumps up for a teabag and goes for a styrofoam cup. He works the Burco and takes the milk out of the fridge, and pours it in while the bag is still in there. If the red roundy yoke off the milk falls in he'll spoon it out and put it back around the lid where it came from. I'd ask him why he does that, but it's better to let on that I'm not watching him. He spoons the teabag out and it drips on the counter on the way to the bin. He'll wipe it up with the cloth and give the tea a stir. The spoon goes in the sink and then he'll touch me on the elbow and he'll hold it up and he has something nearly like a smile for me, half a smile.

On Saturday nights Mum and B go to bed and we go to Athboy. I didn't go during shearing as I wouldn't be able for Sunday but now I can. It is to outside the Darnley Lodge Hotel. The people are old but younger and the language is worse. They can be scary and the way they laugh isn't the same. There's a rush after the pubs shut, and quiet then until when they all come out of the disco in the Darnley. They shout hooray the scutter wagon and chant and howl for curry chips. After they all leave Rory Stone the bouncer comes for a tea and something to eat, and Jerry leans his elbows down on the counter when he's talking to him and Rory Stone leans his shoulder against the side and rests his hand on the bar that props the hatch open.

Jerry says it isn't as suitable and we'll say nothing to my mother but she wouldn't approve and she'd be right not to. The last time there was a big queue and we were very busy, and a man was getting two chicken burgers and two chips and when Jerry put them down and I was asking for the money the man said hold on, I'll have two cans of Club Orange to go with them. Jerry turned round for the two cans and the man looked at me one second nasty and then ran. I pulled at Jerry's shirt and pointed and he went after him and there was cheering and whooping. I didn't know to follow or to stay. I looked out the door that was left open and the man with the burgers tripped and Jerry had him by the shoulder and then he lifted him right off his feet against the wall and held him up by the throat.

When Jerry came back the queue had all stopped laughing and making noise. He gave me a tenner and said for me to give change for two chicken burgers, two chips and two cans, eight sixty. Then he brought the cans and the change over to the man who was sitting on the pavement rubbing his head. Jerry came back and climbed in and shut the door and said who's next and it was still all very quiet. The next man said quarter-pounder and a large chip and Jerry lifted out a basket of chips and threw them into the metal tray. He did up the burger while the man was putting on the salt and vinegar and I got more chips into the chip basket.

It was still all silence, it was so quiet the jenny was very loud, and when Jerry handed the man the quarter-pounder the man said, and actually give me a couple of cans of Club Orange there now I think about it. And Jerry didn't move but looked at him and then the man smiled and said I'm only messing with you and suddenly everyone laughed and the man roared laughing. Jerry smiled and nodded lots and held up one hand and closed his fist and shook it a small bit and then everything went back to normal and everyone was talking again.

Saturday nights driving back is when Jerry gets tired after he's worked since Friday morning and all Friday night and Saturday with no sleep at all. I can't think of other things or questions to ask him or songs to sing, so I whistle as loud as I can in the dark. He says are you whistling to keep me awake and I say no and he says don't worry lad I won't fall asleep, no harm will come to us.

Tonight his eyelids are going down a bit and not going up, and he is driving fast with the window open and the cold night coming in. He keeps taking out the bottle of water he has in the van door and drinking from it. I have some too, just to ask him to pass the bottle so I have something to say. I hold it in two hands in my lap, the water is all empty. It was 7up one time—even the label is gone, only some paper glue left you can feel.

We're on the long hill down to the bad corner by the river—it's too far away to see but I know it's coming from all the times that it is to brake that little bit before and a bit hard because it comes quick. It's where we turn and once we're past it it means we're onto our road and we know we're home. The hill is not steep too much but it's long and straight and you have to take it handy.

We start to go faster when normal times we would be slowing and I can't see if Jerry's eyes are open. I have stopped whistling and I want to ask a question or something but I cannot speak, there is nothing to find to say. There is only the shuttle sound and the speed thundering black outside and Jerry's chin is down and his head is twisted on his neck like the dying lamb in his arms. His head wags and swings and his eyes come all at once a glaring open and are fixed wide. He brakes and brakes hard and we are pouring forward the way the stopping is back.

We are slowed so much we are nearly to a full stop. Jerry blinks and blinks again—he looks out down the black road if something's coming before we go round the bend. He turns to see me and I am here.

He breathes a breath that I can hear and says, many's the time before, when things were bad, I found it hard to slow for this turn. I was often sorely tempted just to leave off on the brake and go into the river. If it wasn't for your mother ... your mother saved my life, young lad, nothing will harm a hair on your head.

I am happy when he says this, Mum is always helping people with remedies and it is a good thing. I have to speak loud because it is important to say something to say that I know.

Her remedies are very good.

He turns to me in the dark as he moves the gearstick, and the headlights run up along the hedgerows. I can see his face in the green light from the dash. He is looking at me, peeking at the road and looking at me.

I look into his eyes and it is like we both know. Maybe it is the rat poison and he was not sick because of the bits of Mum's remedies mixed in. I am scared that he knows and if he knew always.

Can I let you in on a little secret?

I stay looking and he checks the road as we slow for the bend by John Walsh's. On the straight he catches my eye.

Maybe I shouldn't say anything, but to be honest with you I took one dose of the first remedy she gave me and I didn't feel so hot at all. And I never took one bit of it after that.

His eyes are back on the narrow road, and the headlights are making up the new hedges and potholes as we move on. It's the same road as always and I know what's coming but it looks different in the light when you don't expect it.

I am smiling and in my head is floating—tomorrow when I wake up I am going straight to B.

Michaelmas

B has rules for getting in the bath, it's what she does every time and if I do the same thing it will be okay. Once you're sitting in you have to keep your knees up bent and then you have to straighten your legs one by one, very slowly. The bottom half of the leg is under the water like the top half and the knee pokes up above. It is dry and you have to straighten your leg tiny bit by tiny bit so the circle of water becomes smaller and smaller. If you do it very slowly enough there's just a tiny dot of skin left. The water has an edge to it that stops it joining together, and you can see that water has a thickness to it the way a pool of melted wax does when it begins to cool.

I think of people on an island and when the circle closes they all drown. Every time the kettle boils Mum brings it in and pours it in as far away as possible from my toes. She swishes with her hands to move the warm around, one hand bringing the hot up and the other the cold down. The skin goes pink like ham under water in the big saucepan.

I hate the bath. The river is okay and sometimes Mum gives us a bar of soap in the Boyne, and as long as I don't use too much it's okay. I don't trust soap—that brown scummy stuff that collects in the sticks and branches at the edge is other people's old soap and all of that. If it wasn't for soap the water of the Boyne would flow cleanly always.

The worst is the wet hair on my head and I can't see, but I didn't cry last bath so I am not going to cry this time either. I used to try and climb out—in Villiers Square, when we lived by the tinkers, I got tangled in the shower curtain and it all stuck to my body like a burning sheet and I destroyed old Esme's bathroom and she thought there was a pig being killed. But now I'm braver and B sits beside me to hold my hand when Mum does my hair, the worst bit. I squeeze my eyes very tight and I hold my head tipped back, Mum tries to lie me back but I let out a scream and fine fine we'll do it with you sitting up.

I feel the horrid odd wallop of the water going over my head and my hair is all stuck, the scrunchy fingers of the shampoo like a swarm of ants attacking different bits and all over my head, and I feel the trickle of it go in my eye. I squeeze it tighter shut but it's water so it always finds a way through like evil and I shout and shout until they wipe my face with the towel.

Afterwards, under the towel—the towel is so lovely warm from on top of the range, and the fire is so lovely warm crouching beside it—I am naked like I'm dead, as if I've been washed out all parts of me and my skin holds nothing. My fingers are like rotting and the skin is like milk weeks old with a layer of yuck. There's no part of the fields left, my nails are cut shorter down even than the tips of my fingers and they are a shocking white and shocking pink. I close my fists around the corners of the towel and keep covered.

Now doesn't that feel better to be all clean?

I can feel the way my wet hair has been combed, the tugs at my scalp where the knots were still hurt, I can feel the tightness ever of the straight horrible white line where the parting is like a scar on my head. The nails ache at my toes and my fingers where they have been snipped, and my skin is scraped of all its goodness. I have been cut out from the world and am naked, naked like a potato without its skin. I can't reply because I will cry and I'm not going to cry this time.

It must be a little bit nice and refreshing, admit it.

I shake my head at them standing over me with the nasty clean clothes.

Look at that face, Mum says, and her and B scream with laughter together like this is the funniest thing in the world.

Fetch the mirror again to give him another scare.

No, enough B, he's suffered enough.

I don't know why she's still smiling and laughing that I've suffered enough, I can hear her giggling away in the corridor like a ghost.

B holds my pants for me to step into.

You'd better get used to washing. You have to shower every day, and the water is cold, or too hot, sometimes the water is too hot.

B's eyes narrow. Like how hell scalds, that's how hot it is.

But she's smiling so I know she's only joking.

B rolls down the grey socks and holds them open so I can put my feet in easy. When she pulls them up they are nearly to the knee and it is weird. At least now I am not naked, and my skin can begin to go better.

Look at you, says B nodding, her chin in her finger and thumb and her elbow in the cup of her hand—shriven.

What does that mean?

I'm not sure but that's what you look like, ready to meet your maker. Her eyes spark and she smiles, B knows more than me about everything, and if she is smiling everything is okay.

I've never worn a shirt with a collar before. It's brand new and the whiteness of it is like a page blank both sides. It has a thousand pins in it we have to take out, I'm sure we'll forget one and it'll poke into me. The collar rubs against the back of my neck and when I've done up the buttons the front goes far down like a dress. The grey socks are tight around under my knee so as soon as the shirt finishes there's a bit of knee and then sock. The dogs are sniffing around because they know something is happening and they get excited like when we're going to go in the car and go bog jumping and all of that. B laughs at me and goes out with the dogs like she always does before it's time to go.

Mum says it'll be fine tucked in. The shirt sleeves are heavy on my knuckles so I can only see my fingers. The trousers are even darker grey than the socks and the shoes are shiny black and have that horrible stiff new-shoe feel. I walk around to try to soften them, the laces undone making a cat-scratching sound. Mum tells me come back here, and it tickles my ankles when she folds the trousers up inside so it just looks like normal trousers. She laces the shoes for me, nice and tight like the way I like them to be and I say no double knot and she says okay don't worry, now there we are.

Mum stands behind me to do the tie, which is navy blue with thin red stripes slanting on it, you can see the red bright because it's edged in white. She folds my collar around and her fingers feel nice tucking in about my head.

She takes the blazer off the hanger. It is the same as B's with the shield on it and thread animals sewn on like a picture. It's called the crest and Mum doesn't know why. Thankfully it's a hand-me-down one as they are an arm and a leg to buy new. It's a bit big, roomy, and it comes down over my hands like the shirt. I wiggle my fingers with faraway tips sticking out.

Look how smart you are, says Mum, pointing to the mirror.

I look stupid but I don't say anything just stare.

I want to go over to Mrs Lynch to say goodbye first. I'm not to go in, and be quick because we're in a hurry and we have to get on.

I end up having to go in because of the way she lets me, just opening the door and turning for me to follow. But I don't sit up at the table I just say I've come to say goodbye, I'm going off to the boarding school.

I think she will maybe laugh to see me clean and in the clothes and I make a face like I know it is funny too, but Mrs Lynch looks at me and she doesn't laugh at all one bit.

This is the next thing, she says, and she lets her two hands come up like fists and drops them onto her tummy.

This is the next thing now.

This is the next thing is what she says when something bad happens or something she doesn't like. It can be very bad, like when Rosemary ate the poison they had down out in the fields across the road, or only a tiny bit bad, like if there's a bit of frost forecast. But Mrs Lynch takes them all as if they are as bad as each other. She bites her bottom lip and shakes her head and nods and it looks like she wants to cry but won't. Her eyes go hard as pebbles under water. Then she chuckles her laugh and shakes her head some more.

So they're going to send you away, and they're going to make a little gentleman out of you. She puts her hands in her pouch and takes them out again and smooths her apron.

They still haven't copped that it's not you lot in charge anymore.

She bites her lip and it looks like she'll cry again. Her hand is light on my hair.

Sure never mind that, you're a good boy and that's the main thing and your mammy is a fine woman.

I don't say anything.

I don't know how Mrs Lynch knows but she holds me by the shoulder so that I look her in the eye.

Don't you worry about your mammy. Jerry Drain will take good care of her, he's as much of a gentleman as any of them. And your mammy has me looking out for her, the same way she looks out for me.

I give her a look like I know she is joking because she never leaves the house hardly. She lifts her sharp black eyebrows, the grey hairs poking out like wires.

Listen now, who do you think was it suggested Jerry Drain be let those few fields? Ha, ha, ha, she says, ha, ha, ha. Whose idea was it to rent the barn out to him as well, have him going in and out for his few bales of hay? Richard Pink asks me who to lease his land to, and I tell him.

She's smiling again and shaking her head and nodding it too.

Don't forget anything, she says. Do you hear me now?

She takes my face in her soft hands but then holds my chin hard and says it again in bits of one sound.

Do not for get one thing.

Mum takes a green gemstone from her pocket. It's flat and round with a hole in the middle. She holds it up like a card in a game of football and shows me, looking in my eyes so I listen.

This will bring you luck and protect you. There's no need to be worried about anything when you have this on.

There's a leather cord and Mum doubles it to go through the hole and then the ends go through the loop. She ties it at the back, short so it has to be untied to come off, it won't slip over my head. The weight of it is just below the notch of my neck, at the beginning of my chest. She buttons my top button and pulls the tie up tight again, standing back to see.

We should get on and Mum goes to round up B. I say I'll wait for them out at the road and go out to find Gearóid. I meet him coming the other way in the laneway between the sheds.

Ha! The man himself. I was just coming in to say goodbye to you.

I'm meeting Mum and B up at the gate.

Gearóid doesn't say anything and I don't say anything back. We walk together up to the garage and turn there out in front of the house, then he stops.

Don't you worry lad, I'll take care of things here. This is only the next step of your travels. You've been a long way before you came here and you've a long long way to go yet, this is no big deal. No big deal at all.

He kneels down on the ground and I'm taller than him but he grabs me then in a big hug. I feel him scratching on my cheek and hidden in our hug he kisses my ear until it is wet with kisses.

I go slowly down to the trees and Gearóid calls after me.

Work hard, he shouts.

I turn round to him and he lifts his hand right up high, he's going away off towards the garage to get himself set up for the next job.

Every goodbye is the last. I can't have known, but I knew – the day my father walked out and he nodded goodbye to me as he went, the way he turned from me and faced into the day – that he was gone. I felt it that he wasn't ever coming back. I knew it then and I know it still now. And I feel it every time I say goodbye.

That young lad is gone from me now and though I'll see him again. Please God I see him again. He's after saying goodbye to me and I've said goodbye to him.

And one day he'll be told the same thing I was told.

Tá d'athair imithe, agus ní féidir leis teacht ar ais.

And it'll take everything from him, it might even take the language out from his mouth.

Your father is gone, and he can't come back.

I walk out under the trees. I hear the sound of the crows and the leaves already fallen. A whole branch shakes, the leaves ruffling like with the wind. That's a crow flying off from one place and landing in another, none came in from beyond. Some of the fallen leaves look like burnt, there's crispy brown circles on the five big fingers, as if someone's held a flame to each one and that is why they've fallen down. The tree is still green above, but up close the yellows are browning.

Underneath, in the shade, the branches are bare.

There's no grass here, the fallen leaves crackle and slush. There's almost enough cover in them, we could lie down in brown clothes, stay still and never be seen. The dead leaves have spines and ribcages curling, like skeleton boats sunk too long in the water. At the top it's dry but below is mulch, white stems shiny in the dark stew. It wouldn't be comfortable lying still—the wetness would soon soak in.

I catch a chestnut glimpse and find a shell split under a leaf. A chestnut is exciting, the sheen of it, the glow, cold in the white socket but then warm. They should only be opened when they crack a little, otherwise it's too early. The spikes will be ready and waiting and worst of all the chestnut might not be brown. Inside, if the shell is forced, or crushed under a wheel and all of that, split apart too young, it's still white. When they're green they're softer but harder too and don't want to open. There's something wrong looking at a white chestnut, the bright skin stuck damaged to it. You have to wait until they're going yellow, the browner the better.

These ones are more than ready, twins one side of each squashed flat. The shell is brown and dry, even the white inside of it gone brown. Only the nuts are left, their shine like nothing else.

I take one conker out and it goes in my pocket. I rub it with my thumb—the flat shape where it was close squashed up against the other—and look up at the birds from branch to branch.

I wait for the car out by the side of the road, the green stone around my throat.